MEET THE FORTUNES!

Fortune of the Month: Jensen Fortune Chesterfield

Age: 30

Vital statistics: Tall, dark-haired, impeccably groomed—with a swoon-worthy British accent.

Claim to Fame: Sir Jensen is a prince of a man... literally.

Romantic prospects: Stellar, if only he was interested. Sir Jensen keeps his heart locked up as tight as the Crown Jewels.

"That kiss with Amber Rogers? People are making way too much of it. It was all Amber's idea, to distract the paparazzi from my sister. She was just doing a favor for a friend. We are just friends. To think that a down-to-earth cowgirl would get together with a fellow like me is— well, it's pure fiction. A lovely fiction, perhaps. Her long blond hair, those big brown eyes... oh, blimey! We're. Just. Friends."

**THE FORTUNES OF TEXAS:
COWBOY COUNTRY:**
Lassoing hearts f

Dear Reader,

Welcome back to Horseback Hollow, where there's trouble brewing—and plenty of romance, too.

You have no idea how thrilled I was not only to be invited to take part in this new Fortunes of Texas series, but to be asked to write the first book. After being involved in several of these series in the past, the Fortunes and Mendozas have become so real to me they're like family. And I'll bet that's why you've come to love them, too.

It all starts in *A Royal Fortune*, where you'll meet Jensen Fortune Chesterfield. Jensen has just arrived in Horseback Hollow from London to celebrate Christmas with his family and to await the birth of his younger sister's baby. But the handsome yet stoic British nobleman never expected to cross paths with Amber Rogers, a spunky ex-rodeo queen who turns his stuffy heart inside out. In spite of a growing attraction, the pair believe they are just too mismatched to possibly find any middle ground, especially when the paparazzi think they've found one jolly good story. But soul mates come in all shapes and sizes—and from different parts of the globe!

So if you're looking for a little dry English wit versus some down-home Texas "hee-haws" and a heartfelt romance, I think you'll find it as you turn these pages.

Happy reading!

Judy Duarte

A Royal Fortune

Judy Duarte

H·**HARLEQUIN**® SPECIAL EDITION®

Special thanks and acknowledgment to Judy Duarte
for her contribution to the
Fortunes of Texas: Cowboy Country continuity.

ISBN-13: 978-0-373-65860-2

A Royal Fortune

Copyright © 2015 by Harlequin Books S.A.

PLEASE RECYCLE

THIS PRODUCT IS RECYCLABLE

Recycling programs
for this product may
not exist in your area.

HARLEQUIN®
www.Harlequin.com

Printed in U.S.A.

Since 2002, *USA TODAY* bestselling author **Judy Duarte** has written forty books for Harlequin Special Edition, earned two RITA® Award finals, won two Maggies and received a National Reader's Choice Award. When she's not cooped up in her writing cave, she enjoys traveling with her husband and spending quality time with her grandchildren. You can learn more about Judy and her books at her website, JudyDuarte.com, or at Facebook.com/JudyDuarteNovelist.

Books by Judy Duarte

Harlequin Special Edition

Return to Brighton Valley

The Bachelor's Brighton Valley Bride
The Daddy Secret

The Fortunes of Texas:
Welcome to Horseback Hollow

A House Full of Fortunes!

The Fortunes of Texas: Southern Invasion

Marry Me, Mendoza

Byrds of a Feather

Tammy and the Doctor

Brighton Valley Babies

The Cowboy's Family Plan
The Rancher's Hired Fiancée
A Baby Under the Tree

The Fortunes of Texas: Whirlwind Romance

Mendoza's Miracle

Brighton Valley Medical Center

Race to the Altar
His, Hers and...Theirs?
Under the Mistletoe with John Doe

Visit the Author Profile page at Harlequin.com for more titles

To Cindy Kirk, Marie Ferrarella, Michelle Major,
Nancy Robards Thompson and Allison Leigh—
the amazing authors who took part in
The Fortunes of Texas: Cowboy Country.

It was a joy working with each of you. I'd take a trip
back to Horseback Hollow with you anytime!

Chapter One

Jensen Fortune Chesterfield slipped out the back door of the small Texas ranch house in which he was staying, hoping to escape the chattering crowd and to find a little peace and quiet.

Inside, his family had gathered to celebrate Christmas on Boxing Day with their new Texas relatives. But he wasn't in the mood for all the holiday gaiety—and hadn't been since his father died nearly four years ago.

After Sir Simon Chesterfield suffered a fatal heart attack during a polo match, Jensen had been plagued by a bah-humbug mood that began in December and lasted through the better part of January.

In some ways, he wished he'd stayed in England, but his mother wanted him to join her in Horseback Hollow, where his sister Amelia now lived with her husband, Quinn Drummond.

His mother was staying with her sister, while his younger siblings had rooms at a local bed-and-breakfast. Jensen was staying with Amelia and Quinn. The space was a bit tight, but the arrangement suited him. As he stood in the yard, he took in a deep breath and surveyed the grounds. If you removed the vehicles in the drive, the Drummond ranch would've made the perfect Western setting for a cowboy movie. He actually found it quite appealing, but then, he'd always been a fan of classic American Westerns, even the old black-and-white ones he occasionally caught on late-night cable when he couldn't sleep.

Despite his wealthy London upbringing, he liked being in the country. Plus, with him here and Amelia's due date fast approaching, he'd be able to watch over her while Quinn was out working the ranch.

Fortunately, her pregnancy had been uneventful as far as medical concerns. But, emotionally, she'd had a time of it early on, when the paparazzi had pounced on her, making her life miserable. And they'd been especially annoying lately. He wouldn't put it past them to try to infiltrate the family gathering today, which was one reason he was on guard.

He reached inside his pocket and withdrew his gold watch, a habit he'd picked up over the past four years. The treasured heirloom had once belonged to his father, and for some reason, he drew comfort from the weight and the feel of it in his hand.

As the back door squeaked open, Jensen glanced over his shoulder to see his mother stepping out and onto the porch. She was dressed impeccably in a simple forest-green dress and heels, her silver hair coiffed as though her personal stylist had accompanied her on the transatlantic trip to Dallas/Fort Worth and then the quick hop on a charter flight to Lubbock.

"Jensen," she called. "What are you doing outside when the chill is so frightful?"

"I wanted some fresh air." To prove the imaginary excuse, he took a deep breath, relishing the brisk winter breeze.

His mother, Lady Josephine, made her way toward him—no doubt concerned about him distancing himself from the others. But he was in Horseback Hollow, wasn't he? And not out each evening at one of the many parties he'd attend if he was home in London.

Whether she believed it or not, he was actually trying his best to fit in with the numerous Horseback Hollow cousins who were gathered in the house, most of whom he'd only recently met.

His mother frowned—the first sign of distress he'd seen since her arrival in the provincial Western town.

"Is something wrong?" she asked.

"No, not at all." Again he scanned the yard, taking in the barn, the new corral Quinn had built, the old-style windmill that creaked in the breeze. "On the contrary, I was just enjoying the scenery."

"I see," she said, yet her frown failed to lighten. "Are you disappointed about us celebrating together?"

His mother had always known she was adopted, but two years ago, she learned that she'd actually been a triplet. Her brother, James Marshall Fortune, had remained with his birth family. But the two baby girls, Josephine and Jeanne Marie, had been given up and raised in separate households.

"No, Mum. I'm not bothered. I was actually out here counting my blessings."

And if truth be told, that's exactly what he should be doing. He wasn't a loner by nature, but he hated the melancholy that seemed to hover over him during the family get-togethers, especially those associated with the holidays. That's why, at least in December, he preferred to stay in London, where the nightlife, parties and his many social obligations kept him busy and distracted.

She reached out and gave his arm an affectionate squeeze. "We truly have been blessed, haven't we?" Her blue eyes twinkled, and a wistful smile chased away her frown. "I had a lovely childhood, although it was a bit lonely with no siblings. I still can't believe I have a sister and brother—and so many nieces and nephews. Imagine, me—a Yank!"

As if on cue, little Kylie Fortune Jones, Toby and Angie's youngest, popped her head out the door. "It's time to open presents. Are you coming to watch, Aunt Joseph…iiine…I mean, Aunt Lady?"

His mother laughed. "Aunt Josephine will do just fine, love. And we'll be right there."

The title of lady had been honorific, but many of the local Texans were excited to have "royalty" in their midst and tended to make more out of it than Jensen or the rest of the family liked. The press and paparazzi did too, often referring to him and his siblings as sirs, lords or ladies, when neither of their parents' titles had been inherited.

"Isn't Kylie precious?" Josephine said. "I love having young children around again, especially at Christmas."

His mother had always begun her holiday preparations—the shopping, as well as overseeing the decorating and baking—on the first of December. In fact, she'd gone above and beyond to make the holidays happy for all of them.

"I'm glad you can spend this time with your sister," he said.

"So am I."

Still, he found it impossible to explain to an outsider. His mum, who'd grown up on a country estate in England with all the things money could buy, was staying with her newfound sister Jeanne Marie and her husband in a modest ranch house—and clearly delighted with the arrangement. You'd think she was in a five-star hotel with a full staff to cater to her every need.

To be honest, Jensen was a bit surprised by her swift acclimation—culturally speaking. But she was clearly happy. And for that reason, he was happy for her, too.

"Amelia was asking about you," she said.

At that, Jensen's brotherly instincts kicked into full throttle. "Is everything okay?"

"She's fine—other than the usual discomforts to be expected during the ninth month. She asked me to find you because it's nearly time to open the gifts."

Relieved, he nodded. "I'll be right in."

He expected his mum to re-enter the small, two-story house that was busting at the seams with family, leaving him a moment or two longer to relish the quiet.

Instead, she lingered and said, "I wish your father were here."

Jensen's grip on the pocket watch tightened. Sir Simon had been a loving husband and father, and they all missed him terribly.

She sighed, then added, "He would have been a wonderful grandfather."

Jensen slipped his arm around her and pulled her

close to give them both comfort. "You'll be a smashing grandmum, too."

Her eyes glistened. For a moment he feared she would cry and dampen his spirits even worse, but when a smile stretched across her face, he realized grief hadn't made her teary.

"I can hardly wait to hold that baby," she said.

"I'll just be happy when it gets here—and happier if we can keep the bloody photo hounds at bay. They've been sniffing around for a story—or rather, hoping to make up one." Fortunately, Jensen had become adept at avoiding them.

"I do wish you'd come into the house, son. This is the best Christmas I've had since… Well, in years. And I want you to share it with me."

She'd been devastated when his father died and she'd lost her soul mate and the love of her life.

Jensen slipped the gold watch back into his pocket and took her by the arm. "Then let's go inside."

They entered the house through the service porch and headed into the kitchen, where they found his sister making another batch of eggnog. With her long, dark brown hair and doe-like brown eyes, Amelia had always seemed a bit lithe and fragile to him—but more so now that she was due to give birth within the next month or so.

She turned and, upon seeing them, smiled. "Oh, good. Now we're all here."

Well, not all of them. Her once slender waist was as big as the globe in the library back home, reminding Jensen that soon there'd be one more Fortune to add to the world—albeit with the Drummond surname.

"Can I help you with that?" he asked.

"Yes, thank you. I'll tell everyone they can begin passing out their presents now."

Jensen took the bowl and made his way to the living room, which was filled to the brim with relatives, every chair taken, others forced to stand or to find room to sit on the faded rag rug. But apparently, he was the only one who'd found himself on edge.

Jeanne Marie Fortune Jones, who resembled his mother in looks, but not in style, was just as bright eyed and happy as his mum to have the family together. Her husband, Deke, stood by her side, somewhat stoic but with the hint of a grin tugging at his lips.

Their children were all here. Stacey Fortune Jones, along with her fiancé, Colton Foster, kept a close eye on her daughter Piper, who was toddling around the Christmas tree and trying to keep up with her older cousins.

Liam and his fiancée Julia Tierney were posed next to Quinn's upright piano. Jensen suspected someone would suggest they sing a round of Christmas carols before the day was over.

Jude, with his fiancée Gabi Mendoza, stood near the children, all of whom appeared to be on sugar highs. Yet the happy couple held hands and looked on at the festivities as if they couldn't imagine being anywhere else but here.

Even Christopher, who'd been absent from several Horseback Hollow social gatherings last year, was here, along with his fiancée Kinsley Aaron. Apparently, he was back in the family saddle after his rejection of ranch life created discord with his father earlier in the year.

Jensen blew out a sigh. So many engaged couples. Would they all be this happy next year, after their vows were spoken? He hoped so, but he tended to be skeptical about things like that.

Of course, Toby and his wife, Angie, who watched their newly adopted children tear into their gifts, certainly appeared to be as happy as ever.

Rounding out the family gathering were Jensen's brother Charles and his sister Lucie, who were staying in nearby Vicker's Corners at the closest B and B they could find. The two were smiling, but they looked a little uncomfortable among the exuberant American relatives. Jensen wasn't uncomfortable, though. He, better than any of the British Fortunes, probably understood the Texas way of life. He was merely awed by it all.

About that time, his mother approached the serving bowl for a refill of eggnog, which was unusual for a woman who watched her calorie intake. But apparently she was celebrating and throwing caution to the wind.

"It's so good to see you happy, son."

What was she talking about? Had he been smiling?

She slipped an affectionate arm around him. "Have I told you how delighted I am to have so many of my family together?"

The smile, which he must have been wearing, deepened. "Several times in the past hour."

She lifted her free hand and fluttered her fingers in a little wave at her sister, Jeanne Marie, who wore a new pair of her signature stretch-denim jeans and an oversize Christmas-themed jumper.

Again, Jensen was reminded of the sisters' differences. They'd grown up worlds apart—one on an English estate and the other on a small working cattle ranch—something that could be seen easily in their style of dress. Still, they shared many similarities, including a love that knew no bounds.

"This is what it's all about," his mum said. "*Family.*"

Jensen suspected she was talking about more than just a holiday reunion. She'd made no secret of her wish to see him and his siblings settle down. Hopefully, Amelia's baby would take her mind off matchmaking.

But then again, it seemed that everyone else in the room had marriage on their mind. His four engaged cousins had planned a huge wedding for Valentine's Day.

Jensen looked across the room, where Quinn stood next to Amelia, his arm wrapped around her. When she grimaced, Quinn immediately picked up on her discomfort, his expression growing as serious as a first-year pupil meeting his housemaster at Eton.

Amelia smiled, whispered something to her husband and placed his hand over her baby bump. His eyes grew wide and then he smiled, too.

Hopefully Amelia would breeze through labor with no snags or problems. But what if something went wrong during birth? What if…?

Jensen tried to shake his troublesome thoughts. What he really ought to worry about was the press infiltrating the couple's privacy. They'd resorted to all kinds of trickery to learn whether the baby was a girl or boy. But Amelia and Quinn had chosen to be surprised at birth, which none of the reporters believed.

A rap sounded at the door just as laughter burst out at something Toby's precocious daughter had said to her red-haired brother.

Jensen heard another noise, although no one else seemed to take note of it. Had someone knocked?

* * *

Amber Rogers stood on the Drummonds' front porch and rapped on the door again. She'd driven to the Rocking U Ranch to deliver a gift for Amelia, Quinn's new wife. It was a handmade baby blanket, although the sections Amber had quilted weren't as neatly stitched as Gram's.

But it was the thought that counted, right?

There were a whole slew of cars parked outside and a god-awful commotion going on inside the house, but apparently no one had heard her knock. So she rang the bell.

Moments later, a tall and sophisticated stranger swung open the door. He was wearing a well-tailored suit and tie—something so out of place and unexpected on a small Texas ranch that it caught her off guard and made her think about the back-to-back episodes of *Downton Abbey* she'd been watching with Gram.

Surely Lady Josephine hadn't brought along her butler and the entire Chesterfield Estate staff.

But then she realized exactly where she'd seen the drop-dead gorgeous guy before—on the front page of a tabloid down at the Superette—and she swallowed. Hard.

Before she could think better of it, she blurted out, "Oh, it's you."

"I beg your pardon?" he said in a rich British accent.

Amber cringed inwardly. Obviously they'd never met, and she'd just implied that they had. Why did she always have to stick her foot in her mouth?

She opened her lips to apologize, but she merely stammered instead, her cheeks warming.

Dang. She could be such a goof at times.

"What do you want?" he asked—and not very nicely.

This wasn't going at all well.

She lifted the wrapped gift. "I'm sorry. I brought this for Amelia…um…Mrs. Drummond…or should I call her Lady Amelia?"

Amber hadn't meant to sound so uncertain, but Sir Jensen's good looks, royal appearance and hoity-toity attitude had nearly knocked her out of her cowboy boots.

His eyes narrowed. "Do you *know* Mrs. Drummond?"

"Not really. I just—" Before she could explain that she'd only recently moved back home to Horseback Hollow, and that she was Quinn Drummond's neighbor, the stuffy Brit snatched her package right out of her hands.

"I'll see that she gets it," he said. Then he shut the door right in her face.

Of all the nerve. He'd just dismissed her! She had half a notion to lean on the bell until someone else came to the door, someone who knew her. But she merely stood there, gaping, dumbfounded by the man's rudeness.

Three seconds later—and yes, *seconds* because she'd counted them off as an attempt to hold her temper—the door swung open again. This time, Jeanne Marie peered out and broke into a smile. "Hi, sweetie. Come on in."

Amber hesitated. "I'm not so sure I should." Nor did she want to. Her mother had been longtime friends with Jeanne Marie, but even the woman's warm welcome couldn't lessen the insult of the snobby man's bad manners. What a jerk.

"Don't pay any mind to Jensen. He's just an overprotective big brother."

This was Horseback Hollow—not a Revolutionary War battlefield. What possible threat could Amber be? She was just trying to be neighborly. But she held her tongue before she popped off with something rude herself. Instead, she would graciously drop off the gift and make a proper excuse to leave. Once she'd shut the door, she could turn on her booted heel and stomp off. She'd never have to step foot on the Drummond place until the entire British side of the family—all except Amelia, of course—went back to their side of the pond.

Jeanne Marie took her hand and pulled her into the midst of the bustling holiday revelers. "Look who's here, everybody!"

Amber never had been what you'd call shy. In fact, as a former rodeo queen and barrel racer, she was used to riding into an arena full speed with her flag flying. But she hadn't expected to walk into a big ol' family Christmas celebration.

Heck fire. Yesterday was the twenty-fifth. She'd known better than to show up then.

"I'm sorry," she said. "I hadn't meant to horn in on your family celebration. I thought by waiting until the twenty-sixth, I'd miss it."

"With everyone having so many family gatherings to attend, this seemed to be the easiest way to get together."

Amber glanced at Jensen, who'd answered the door like a jerk and now appeared rather sheepish. Well, *bully* for that. It served him right for being such a snob.

Amber knew how some of the wealthy British behaved, thanks to Gram's recent addiction to the *Downton Abbey* series. And Jensen reminded her of the snooty upper crust.

Jensen approached Amber and reached out his hand in greeting, his sheepish expression morphing into one that was almost...dashing. "I'm sorry for being rude when I answered the door. We've been bombarded by some rather innovative members of the press, as well as the paparazzi lately, and I was merely trying to ward them off at the pass. Allow me to properly introduce myself. I'm Jensen, Amelia's older brother."

If Amelia's handsome big brother thought that she'd acted like a fool at the royal sight of him, at least he was gentlemanly enough not to mention it.

And while Amber had always had a stubborn streak, she'd never been one to hold a grudge. Besides, it was the Christmas season—God rest ye merry gentlemen and all of that.

So she took his hand and gave it a hearty shake. "Apology accepted. We own a spread down the road a piece."

"Do you raise cattle—like Quinn?" he asked.

"No. We breed and train cutting horses."

"Really?" He seemed to perk up and ease closer. And he held her hand a moment longer. "I'd be interested in seeing your operation sometime."

No kidding? Where did that come from? Not that she'd object. It's just that...well, he'd gone from stuffy to friendly in zero to sixty, and she wasn't quite sure what to make of it. Nor was she sure what to make of the warmth of his touch.

"Sure," she said, withdrawing her hand from his. "You can come out for a visit. I'd be happy to give you a tour."

"Would tomorrow be convenient?"

So soon?

She shook off her momentary surprise. "That's fine. The Broken R is about four miles down the road. There's a big green John Deere mailbox in front of a white wrought-iron gate. You can't miss it."

"Would there be a more suitable time for my visit?"

My, the man was certainly formal. And persistent. But then again, he was probably used to getting his way. With the ladies, too, no doubt. She smiled. "This is Texas. Our ranches are always open and ready to receive company. How about nine? Or is that too early for you?"

"I'm up bright and early. So that's not a problem."

A smile stole across her face. She wondered what time the royals considered early. She and every rancher she knew usually woke before dawn.

"So," she said, "the press has been pestering y'all?"

"Like hounds on a fox. We've grown up with it, so we usually take it in stride. But they've taken great pleasure in the fact that Amelia has fallen in love with a cowboy. And now that she's settled in Horseback Hollow and is expecting a baby, they've been making it extremely difficult on her."

No wonder he'd thought Amber was up to something when she'd rang the bell.

"In fact," Jensen said, "now that the birth is so close at hand, they've been especially wily and persistent."

"Just so they can take photographs?" she asked.

"Yes, and to be the first to report whether the new little one is a boy or a girl."

Amber, who'd always been as curious as she'd been stubborn couldn't help but turn to the handsome British royal and ask, "Which is it going to be?"

"Even if I knew, I wouldn't breathe a word of the secret. But Amelia and Quinn have decided to be surprised." Jensen crossed his arms and tossed her a cocky smile, reminding her of a Cheshire cat and making her heart scamper.

Fortunately, before she had to decide what to do about it, Jeanne Marie approached. "Can I get either of you a cup of coffee? Or maybe you'd rather have Jensen pour you some of Amelia's eggnog? You can have it with rum or without."

"You might fancy a cup with rum," Jensen said. "It's quite good. And a holiday tradition in our family. I'll pour you a spot."

Amber thanked him.

"It's been fun blending our holiday traditions," Jeanne Marie added.

"I guess change isn't always a bad thing." Amber wished she would eventually come to believe that herself.

Jeanne Marie sighed. "I don't know about that. When it comes to family, it's been fun. But not when it comes to our town and community."

"Are you talking about Cowboy Country USA?" Amber knew where Jeanne Marie was going with that. The town had seemed to split in its support of the new Western theme park that was being built near Vicker's Corners. Some thought it would draw tourists and business to Horseback Hollow and others were staunchly against its construction because they feared it would make a mockery of the Western life they held dear.

"Now, I'm not one to get political," Jeanne Marie said. "And I'm not about to make a fuss down at city hall or give speeches in Town Square on Founder's Day. But I like Horseback Hollow just the way it is."

Amber understood her concern—and that of the others, too. But she was excited to have an amusement park so close to home. She loved roller coasters and thought it would be cool to show the tourists from the rest of America how their country counterparts lived.

She'd also been approached by the casting department of Moore Entertainment about starring in their Wild West Show. And she was going to accept the offer because it would provide her with an opportunity to rope and ride again in an arena, while not having to leave Gram to run the ranch alone. She hadn't told anyone, though. No need to risk getting run out of town on a rail.

Besides, she wouldn't hurt Jeanne Marie for the world. The woman had become a second mother to her after her own mama had passed.

When Jensen returned, Jeanne Marie and Lady Josephine excused themselves and went to find seats closer to all the holiday activity.

"Here you go, Miss…" Jensen paused as he handed Amber a glass of eggnog, along with a holiday napkin. "I'm afraid I didn't catch your last name."

"It's Rogers," she said, as she took the drink and thanked him.

Jensen—Lordy, the man was handsome—tossed her an earth-tilting grin. "Are you any relation to Roy?"

"You mean Rod, who owns the R and J Auto Body in Vicker's Corners? No, I'm afraid not."

"Actually," he said, "I was referring to Roy Rogers, the old-time movie star."

Amber stole a glance at the Brit. Who in America, especially the state of Texas, wouldn't know who Roy Rogers was? She just hadn't expected Jensen to. But rather than point out their obvious cultural differences, she said, "I'm afraid that was a bit before my time."

"It's before mine, as well. But since I'm an American Western film buff, I'm familiar with all the old movie stars, such as Tom Mix, Randolph Scott, John Wayne..."

She crossed her arms and shot him a playful grin. "So you assumed that, just because I'm a cowgirl, that I should be familiar with all things Western, even from sixty and seventy years ago?" He probably also thought she sang on her horse as she cantered along in her fringed pink vest à la Dale Evans.

"I'm sorry. It appears that I'm making all kinds of false assumptions today."

"Apparently so. But you don't have to be so formal. You can call me Amber."

"Well, Miss Amber Rogers, if you'll excuse me, it looks like that eggnog needs to be replenished again."

That seemed an odd job for a man—especially a fancy-pants one like him, who was just a guest in the house anyway. Was he trying to get away from her?

As much as she'd wanted to avoid him in the past, she was a bit sorry to see him go. He was actually charming—when he wanted to be.

As he made his way to the punch bowl, which was indeed nearly empty, he was stopped several times along the way—first by one of his cousins, then by one of the children. He would smile and comment, yet he appeared to hold back, to remain somewhat aloof.

He'd seemed to lower his guard with her, though, but just for a moment. And only when they'd talked about old movies and horses.

She couldn't help watching as he moved through the

house, chatting with his family, yet milling about looking as neat and formal as his professionally pressed suit.

Jensen was a looker—if you liked the fancy and stylish kind of man who could grace the cover of a men's fashion magazine.

Of course, she'd always favored the rugged outdoorsman, like cowboys and ranchers. Real men, not city boys.

Still, Jensen Fortune Chesterfield was a sight to behold—and to study, to admire, as long as he wasn't aware of her interest.

Funny thing, though. For a man who seemed to have it all together—amazing good looks, a boatload of money, a royal family and position—he seemed to distance himself from the others.

But then again, she could see why someone as stuffy as him would be a loner. And she couldn't help feeling a bit sorry for him.

There was something about Jensen that gave her a feeling of…well, she couldn't quite put her finger on it. But it was a feeling she just couldn't quite name or shake.

It was as if she knew him—or was destined to know him.

Hmm. Now *that* was weird. Because it made zero sense. He was British royalty and wool suits. And she was one hundred percent Texas cowgirl and worn jeans. They were as ill-suited as a cutting horse at the Grand National.

You'd think that would be the end of it. But oh, no. He'd gone and invited himself out to the Broken R tomorrow. And like the goof that she was, she'd agreed to a tour. So she was stuck seeing him again.

But after that, she'd cut herself out of the herd and make a quick getaway. Because what possible good could come of a friendship between a down-home country girl and the lord of the manor?

Chapter Two

Amber had expected to see Jensen show up at the Broken R the next morning since he'd asked if he could see her breeding operation. But she'd thought he'd probably take his jolly good time, as the aristocracy was prone to do, and arrive late, driving a borrowed ranch truck, kicking up dust and trying to get used to having the steering wheel on the correct side of the vehicle.

What she hadn't expected to see was him all decked out in English riding clothes and mounted on Trail Blazer, the gelding Quinn Drummond had recently purchased from her.

Still, here he was. And she'd promised to give him a tour. So she walked down the porch steps, carrying a mug of fresh-brewed coffee, and waved as he rode up.

When he dismounted in a swift, fluid motion, she sucked in her breath at the way his jodhpurs hugged his muscular legs.

Yet she stifled a grin, too. Who the heck wore fancy English riding britches in Horseback Hollow?

"Hi," she said, which was about all she could muster, as she watched him stride toward her in a pair of swanky brown equestrian boots.

Did he think she'd invited him over to play polo? If so, he was as out of place on the Broken R as she would have been sipping tea in Buckingham Palace.

And speaking of being out of place, so was that little flutter that was racing up and down her spine.

He held the horse's reins in one hand and reached out the other to her in greeting. "Good morning."

Well, dang. The gent was certainly formal. She shifted the steaming mug to her left hand and accepted his handshake. But the moment his fingers wrapped around hers, her pulse rate spiked.

Then, upon his release, which was slow and drawn out, that little flutter took off like a flock of turtledoves, and she nearly dropped her coffee on the ground.

"I hope I'm not too early," he said.

He was too everything. Too early, too formal, too good-looking. But her grandmother had raised her to be a gracious hostess, and she didn't give voice to her racing thoughts. "Of course not. Can I get you a cup of coffee? Or tea? You guys probably prefer tea, right?"

"We guys?"

"You Brits."

He smiled and gave her a slight nod of his head. "Actually, I was hoping for a nice pot of chicory cooked over a campfire. That's what you country-and-western 'guys' drink, correct?"

The glint of amusement in his eyes sent her already soaring pulse rate into a loop de loop, but she reined it back down to earth the best she could and tossed him a smile of her own. "Fair enough. I guess we probably shouldn't make assumptions about each other. So…? Coffee or tea?"

"Neither, thank you. Amelia cooked a huge breakfast this morning. I believe she's going through what the maternity experts call 'the nesting period.' She can't stop cleaning and organizing and freezing big pans of food Quinn refers to as casseroles."

Amber laughed at the animated confusion in Jensen's eyes. "I've heard about nesting. I would imagine the responsibility of bringing another life into the world would be a little overwhelming. She probably just wants to get everything in order."

"I take it you don't have children?" Jensen glanced down at her left hand.

She moved the mug handle around, not wanting to draw attention to the fact that her ring finger was very much unadorned.

"Nope," she said. "No kids. But maybe someday."

"My aunt Jeanne Marie said you live here with your grandmother?"

"Yes, it's just me and Gram." She dumped the rest of her coffee into a shrub near the barn, then set the mug on the fence post. "Actually, I only moved back to Horseback Hollow a few months ago."

"Where were you living before that?"

My, he was certainly full of questions for a man who'd closed the door in her face when he'd thought she'd been a nosy reporter. She wondered how he'd like a taste of his own medicine. But she didn't have anything to hide. Well, other than her possible job with Cowboy Country USA. But if that came to be, and it certainly looked promising, it would soon be out in the open as front-page news for the *Cross Town Crier*, the county weekly paper. And boy, was she dreading that day...

"I traveled around," she admitted. "I was on the professional rodeo circuit for a couple of years and spent most of the time living out of a trailer."

She waited for him to lift his snooty British nose at that revelation, but he just nodded his head as if he'd expected her response.

"Like a caravan?" he asked.

"A what?"

"A *caravan*. Isn't that what you Americans call a recreational vehicle?"

"I guess—if it's a whole bunch of them. Sometimes we stayed in motels or would bunk at a friend's ranch. It's a far cry from the glamorous world you're probably used to living in. But I loved the rodeo life—the traveling and the camaraderie." In fact, after only a few months away, she was already missing it.

"It sounds quite exciting, actually. Like Dale Evans, Queen of the West."

Was he comparing her to a movie star from the fifties? Seriously?

"Dale Evans?" she asked.

He nodded, and his dark brows lifted as if he was... well, if not intrigued, then definitely interested.

She shrugged. "I guess it was kind of like that, but with faster riding and less singing."

He smiled. "I actually have a film library and collect all the classic American Westerns and some documentaries. I've even watched some of the rodeos on television. But besides an appreciation for thoroughbred racing—especially the Kentucky Derby—I'm afraid my knowledge of other American horsing sports is some-what limited."

The tension in Amber's shoulders eased. So that's why he was here. He really *was* a greenhorn, inter-ested in the Wild West. And if he was still going to be in town this summer, when Cowboy Country USA opened for business, he'd probably be the first in line to buy a front-row seat.

Well, she could deal with that kind of fan. And while his style of dress was better suited to a polite game of polo than to bronc busting, she'd give him a tour, just as she'd promised.

She rubbed the bay gelding's nose. "So what do you think of Trail Blazer? Though I realize you're more into the English style of riding."

"He's a fine horse. Quinn said your grandfather trained him."

"That's right. Trail Blazer is one of the last colts out of Moonshine, my pop's pride and joy. The other is Lady Sybil. She's one of our more spirited fillies."

"Lady Sybil? As in the character from *Downton Abbey*?" He arched his brow.

Amber's cheeks warmed at the connection. The last thing she wanted was for Jensen to think she was some sort of British noble wannabe like a few of the other Horseback Hollow residents. But since he was such a Western movie buff, maybe he wouldn't judge her too harshly. "Gram is a big fan of the show. Anyway, come on into the stable and you can meet her."

"Lady Sybil or your grandmother?"

Amber laughed as Jensen followed, the bay gelding trailing behind him. "No, Gram went to Vicker's Corners this morning to meet with her quilting club. And the rest of the hands are still off for the holidays. It's just me, you and the horses."

As soon as the words were out of her mouth, she wanted to snatch them back. "What I meant was that nobody else is here to bother…I mean, we're alone… Oh, heck. What I'm trying to say is that there's no reason to keep me from showing you around. Why don't we start in the barn?"

She kept walking, not wanting to turn and face him since the blush in her cheeks had probably deepened to the exact shade of red in her plaid shirt. Fortunately, the cool confines of the stable and its familiar smell of straw and horses brought her back to her senses and provided a better state of mind.

For the next thirty minutes, Amber showed him the broodmares and several new foals. "Almost all of the mares were bred and trained on our ranch. We ride and work with them, so we know their strengths and weaknesses. We're also honest and fair. If we don't have what a buyer is looking for, we can usually refer them to another breeder or trainer."

"I know horses and can see that you have some good quality stock here."

She thanked him, then led him out of the barn. While he waited near the outside corral, Amber saddled Lady Sybil, the spunky bay filly she was still training—and not planning to sell, although there'd been several substantial offers already.

"I appreciate you taking the time to give me a tour," Jensen said. "You must be especially busy with your staff on holiday."

"It's not too bad. We planned ahead and took care of all the major chores before they left."

"If there's something I can do to help," he said, "just let me know. Quinn is staying close to the house this weekend, so I have some free time."

Jensen might be an accomplished rider, but she couldn't see him helping out on the Broken R.

"Thanks for the offer," she said. "I'll keep that in mind."

He remounted Trail Blazer and together they set off to see the rest of the ranch.

Throughout their morning ride, he asked polite but inquisitive questions about their operation. It was easy to see that he had an avid interest in the ranch, although several times, she'd caught him watching her in a way that had her zinging and pinging all over.

She'd stolen a few glances his way, too. But that was to be expected. After all, the Brit was so foreign to her, it was no wonder she couldn't keep her eyes off him.

Right? That's all it was. Jensen could have been from another planet—or even another century, like the one in which Jane Austen had lived. The early 1800s, if Amber remembered what she'd learned in her English Lit class.

"You have a lovely piece of land," he said. "And an impressive operation."

"Thank you. It's been in the family for generations."

As they made their way back to the stables after their tour, it was just about noon. She wondered if she ought to ask him if he'd like a sandwich—or if she ought to send him on his way.

Seemingly he was in no hurry to leave because he dismounted first and tied up his horse while she rode Lady Sybil into the paddock.

So, now what?

She bit down on her bottom lip as she slowed her mount, giving a lunch invitation some thought, when a rumble grew in the distance.

Lady Sybil whinnied.

"Easy, girl." Amber tightened her grip on the reins and stroked the filly's neck, but with the approaching engine's roar, the horse grew more apprehensive.

A loud green car churned up a cloud of dust as it tore down the long driveway toward the ranch house, fishtailing its way toward them.

Lady Sybil whinnied again, tossing her head back and forth. Amber leaned low over the agitated animal's neck to avoid getting thrown.

Jensen jumped over the railing and ran to her side. Obviously, he didn't realize that Amber was perfectly capable of handling the horse—or used to picking herself up after a fall—because he grabbed the horse's bridle and murmured to Sybil in his soft English accent.

The horse stilled, and Amber began to dismount. But the darned vehicle backfired and the mare bolted to the right, which threw Amber off balance.

She stumbled toward Jensen, and he slipped an arm around her, steadying her just as effectively as he'd steadied the filly.

Yet as his fingertips dug into her waist, sending a bolt of heat to her core, he unraveled just about everything else holding her together, and she darn near dropped the reins.

Thank goodness he had a hold of them, too. And her.

When he looked at her, assessing her with eyes the color of fine Texas bourbon, their faces just inches apart, her breath caught and her lips parted. But before

Amber could either think or blink, Lady Sybil tossed her head once more, and she came to her senses, pulled away and took control of the horse, just as the roaring muscle car parked in front of the house.

A dust cloud swirled around the windows, making it difficult to see who was inside, but there were two of them—a man and a woman. When the engine shut off, the driver's door opened, releasing the big band sounds of the Glenn Miller Orchestra.

Uh-oh. That explained it all. Gram had come home with that man again.

But this time, there was an upside. At least, Amber had an excuse to put some distance between her wacky hormones and the fancy British nobleman who'd aroused them.

For the briefest of moments, while Jensen had rushed to Amber's assistance, something had passed between them—an intimacy that had shocked the living daylights out of him.

The minute his hand slid around her waist, he couldn't help pulling her closer—and not just in an attempt to save life and limb. Then, when her lips parted, there'd been a moment—a single heartbeat, actually—when he'd been sorely tempted to kiss her.

Amber must have felt it, too, because she'd had such a lovely expression of bewilderment—that is, until Lady Sybil and the big green machine had put a stop to it all and reality had set in.

The driver of the green Dodge Charger, a squat older gent in his early eighties, climbed out of the car and yelled over the sound of swing music, "I can't figure out how to turn this dadgummed i-radio off."

Then he reached back into the car, took the hand of the lady who'd accompanied him and helped her to slide across the bench seat and exit through the driver's door.

But rather than calling it a day, the older gent spun the woman in his arms and lowered her into a graceful dip that should have only been attempted by the most agile of professional dancers.

Jensen found it all rather amusing.

Apparently Amber didn't because she handed him Lady Sybil's reins, then strode across the yard, reached inside the vehicle and disconnected a cord, ending the song, as well as the impromptu dance. "What are you doing?"

"Practicing our moves for the upcoming dance contest at the Moose Lodge," the elderly gent said. "I'm trying to talk Helen into competing with me, instead of with Harold Witherspoon, who don't stand a chance of winning, even with a woman as pretty as Helen in his arms."

Amber shifted her weight to one booted foot. "Gram, I thought you and Mary Trimble went to have breakfast with your quilting group."

The older lady, who wore a green floral dress and a cream-colored sweater, turned to her granddaughter with flushed cheeks and a pleasant smile. "We did have breakfast, honey. But on the way, we learned that Martha Bradshaw's relatives are all still staying at her house, which is where we usually go. So the group had a change of plans, and we decided to move over to the VFW instead. I ran into Elmer Murdock there, and he offered to give me a ride home so Mary wouldn't have to."

Amber's grandmother, whose steel-gray hair had

been woven into a French twist, fingered the side of her head and tucked a loose strand behind her ear before addressing Jensen. "I'm Helen Rogers. I recognize the horse you're riding, but I don't believe you and I have met."

"It's a pleasure to meet you, ma'am. I'm Jensen Fortune Chesterfield." Then he turned to her companion.

The short, elderly man with a gray buzz cut reached out a weathered hand and gave Jensen a firm handshake. "Elmer Murdock, United States Marine Corps, retired."

Jensen glanced at Amber, who didn't look too pleased with the newcomer's arrival.

"You Jeanne Marie and Deke's nephew?" Mr. Murdock asked him.

"Yes. I'm in town staying with my sister, Amelia."

The man's clear blue eyes traveled up and down, studying Jensen hard, but not in a threatening manner. "Those are some pretty fancy riding breeches."

"Thank you."

"Where'd you find them? Might get me a pair like that."

"Actually, I purchased them at a shop in Windsor."

"Humph. That figures. You being one of them Fortunes from England and all." Mr. Murdock crossed his arms, gave a little nod, then rocked back and forth. "You got any relatives that fought in the RAF?"

"Yes, sir. My father was a pilot in the RAF."

"You don't say." Mr. Murdock stroked his chin. "He see any action in the war?"

"Which war?"

"Any of 'em. Personally, I was too young to fight the Germans. I had to earn my stripes over in Korea. But my older brother Chester went over early and helped get you boys out of that pickle in dubya dubya two."

Clearly, Elmer Murdock was quite the spitfire, but Jensen was used to the bravado of elderly soldiers when it came to World War II and their role in it. "Then I thank both you and your brother for your service."

"You're welcome. The US of A has no match on the battlefield, which some of your kin found out for themselves back during the Revolutionary War."

"Jensen," Mrs. Rogers said, before the men lapsed into a patriotic rivalry, "I was just about to fix lunch. I hope you'll join us."

Jensen glanced at Amber, who still held Mr. Murdock's music device in her hand. A frown marred her pretty face, but he didn't think it was because he'd been invited to stay. Instead, he had a feeling it was because her grandmother had included Mr. Murdock.

And while Jensen probably ought to gracefully decline, he remembered hearing the ingredients of the franks and tots casserole Amelia planned to make for lunch, doubling the recipe so she could freeze the leftovers. Suspecting his odds for a tasty meal would be much better here on the Broken R, he said, "Thank you, Mrs. Rogers. I'd like that."

Besides, he'd enjoyed his tour of the ranch and had found Amber even more intriguing. The cowgirl had been so animated when she'd explained their operation, and when she'd talked about animal husbandry, it had sounded as if she had an advanced degree. He couldn't help wanting to spend more time with her.

"I'm so happy you'll be joining us." Mrs. Rogers flashed a smile at her friend, then hurried into the house.

Amber walked around the front of the early model Dodge Charger, assessing the vehicle that had delivered her grandmother home from Vicker's Corners. "Is this your car, Mr. Murdock?"

"Sure is. I'm getting this beauty ready for the classic car show me and some of the boys down at the VFW are planning to put on next fall. We're calling it Cruisin' Vicker's. All the cars have to be built in 1975 or earlier."

While Jensen didn't think this old heap would win any competitions, he kept his opinion to himself.

"The cars don't have to be American made," Murdock added with a sly nod at Jensen. "So if you want to ship one of your fancy MGs or Jaguars this way, you can."

"That's kind of you to invite me," Jensen said, "but I'll be in town only for a short duration."

"Well, hopefully you'll stick around for a few more weeks." The old man patted the hood of the car. "I should have the new paint job done by then, and Rod down at R and J Auto Body promised he'd order a passenger-side door, too, since I can't get the fool thing to open."

"Rod Rogers?" Jensen asked, letting the old man know that he was picking up on a few names and business owners in the area.

"Yup. That's him."

"I don't suppose he's any relation to Roy Rogers," Jensen said, more to tease Amber than anything.

"Shoot, no," Murdock said. "But he might be related to Amber and Helen."

Jensen turned back to the cowgirl he'd likened to Dale Evans, the one who'd told him she wasn't related to either man, and winked.

"No," she said. "I'm not related to Rod Rogers, the car mechanic, or to the singing cowboy."

"Well, I'd rather be related to Rod any day over that mansy pansy Roy Rogers," Mr. Murdock said.

"Really?" Jensen asked, "What's wrong with Roy? I like the Western films he made."

"Westerns?" Murdock humphed. "If you wanna watch an authentic Western, you go see something by John Wayne. Now there's a real actor. 'Course, I like him in *The Green Berets* on account of that's a good war movie, and I'm a military man myself."

Amber rolled her eyes just as her grandmother stepped onto the porch. "Elmer, can you come help me with the sweet tea?"

"'Scuse me, you two. I gotta go help sweeten Helen up." He raised his weathered hands in a sign of surrender. "What can I say? The woman sure does love my sweet tea."

Mr. Murdock lumbered toward the house and Amber shook her head.

When he was out of earshot, Jensen said, "I take it you're not a fan of Mr. Murdock."

"I like him just fine. I've known him all my life. He's a funny old codger, and I usually get a kick out of being around him. But now that he's been spending more time with Gram, it just doesn't feel right."

"What do you mean?"

"It's not that I don't want my grandmother to be happy. I do. But it's going to take a special man to take my pop's place. And I just don't think there's one out there who won't disappoint her."

Or perhaps disappoint Amber?

In all honesty, Jensen knew just how she felt. His

mother had lost her true love and soul mate when his father passed away, and he doubted she'd ever find another man to take his place.

"Besides," Amber said, "those two are so different from each other. They have nothing in common and are complete opposites. It would never work out."

"Are you sure about that?" Jensen asked. "I know Mr. Murdock seems a little…"

"Rough around the edges?" Amber said.

"Perhaps a bit. He's certainly colorful."

"Yes, and Gram is a quiet sort. She likes to stay home and bake and sew. Her idea of excitement is going to church or to an occasional movie in Vicker's Corners. But then in walks Elmer Murdock—or should I say, 'in charges Elmer.' And now she's doing all kinds of wild and crazy things."

"Like what?"

"Going on hikes with backpacks—and just because he'd made a bet with some buddy that he could get Helen Rogers to agree to go with them."

"And Mr. Murdock was able to talk her into it?" If that was so, then maybe the old girl had more feelings for him than Amber realized.

"Elmer told her that it was a charity event with all the proceeds going to the Wounded Warrior Project."

"He lied to her?"

"Elmer Murdock may be a lot of things," Amber said. "Eccentric and even annoying at times. But you'll never meet a man more patriotic and more supportive of our troops and military. He'd never make light of something like that. The event was sponsored by the Moose Lodge. He won the bet and even turned over the five dollars to the charity, as well."

"I'm not sure I—"

Amber slapped her hands on her hips. "My gram is seventy-five years old, Jensen. She shouldn't be carrying backpacks and going on hikes with a bunch of military veterans as if they were picnics in the park."

It sounded as though Mrs. Rogers might have enjoyed the outing, but Jensen didn't mention it. Not when Amber was so clearly miffed.

And miffed indeed. A fire—sparked by fierce loyalty and compassion, no doubt—lit her eyes and revealed her true spirit.

A smile tugged at his lips. He'd never much liked to see a woman annoyed, but this one was actually quite lovely—perhaps because her annoyance wasn't directed at him.

"And now this." Amber swept her hand across the length of the muscle car. "What in the world was Gram doing, blowing around town in that green death machine?"

Poor Mr. Murdock. Amber wasn't going to make this courtship easy for him.

"Perhaps she's just having a bit of fun and it will all blow over soon."

Amber let out a sigh. "I hope you're right."

When she looked up at him with soulful brown eyes, Jensen was taken aback—transported, actually—to that moment when Murdock arrived and Lady Sybil had acted up. When Jensen had stepped in to help Amber dismount and briefly thought of kissing her.

But that wouldn't do.

It wouldn't do at *all*.

"Well, we'd better put the horses away," Amber said. "Then I'll help Gram get lunch on the table."

It would seem that Mrs. Rogers already had help with that task, but Jensen kept his thoughts to himself. Instead, he watched the sexy cowgirl walk toward the barn, enjoying the way her denim jeans curved on her derriere.

He had to admit that Mrs. Rogers and Mr. Murdock didn't seem any more suited for each other than he and Amber were.

Maybe Amber had realized his interest in her and this was her way of letting him know that she didn't believe in the old adage that opposites attract.

If so, that was too bad.

Physically, Jensen was captivated by the cowgirl, but he was a rational man who understood that duty came first. And right now, his duty was to his family.

Besides, in a few weeks, six at the most, he'd be back in London, which was in an entirely different universe than Horseback Hollow. And he wouldn't think of the beautiful Amber Rogers again.

Unfortunately, for the time being, he feared that he wouldn't be able to think of anything else.

Chapter Three

Lunch went much better than Amber had expected—thanks in large part to Jensen's presence. The Brit had a dry wit and a way of making everyone feel comfortable, a skill he must have perfected as an aristocrat attending various charity events and rubbing elbows with the lower classes. Not that she knew anything about the life he actually led, but she did glance at the headlines of the tabloids whenever she stood in the checkout line of the Superette, and so his social activities were no big secret, even if he didn't have an official royal title.

Amber had expected the meal to be awkward, but unlike yesterday, Jensen hadn't seemed the least bit snobbish today.

"Thank you for a lovely meal," he said, as he rose from the table. "You're a wonderful cook, Mrs. Rogers. I enjoyed that chicken salad. And your chocolate cake was one of the best I've ever had."

"Why, thank you," Gram said. "I'm glad you liked it. But please, call me Helen."

"All right, I will." He then reached across the table and shook Elmer's hand. "It was a pleasure, Mr. Murdock. Good luck refurbishing that car. I hope you win the competition."

Elmer stood as tall as his five-foot-four-inch frame would allow. "And just so you know, there's been some talk about you English taking over Horseback Hollow. Some are downright pleased and giddy about it, while others are fretting about a British invasion. But I'll have you know, you're A-OK in my book."

Jensen chuckled. "I'm pleased to hear that."

"Come on," Amber said. "I'll walk you outside."

Once they left the house and were out of earshot, she blew out a sigh. "I hope that wasn't too trying for you."

"Actually, I enjoyed myself. And I wasn't just being polite. Your grandmother is a good cook."

"I think so, too. But a man like you has eaten meals from the best chefs all over the world. So I have a feeling you've just gotten your fill of casseroles lately."

He laughed—a hearty, resonant sound that lifted her spirits, making her forget all about the green Charger parked near the house or the man inside who'd insisted upon helping Gram with the dishes.

"You have a point," Jensen said. "But that chicken salad was excellent. And so was the chocolate cake, which could rival any I've ever had the pleasure to eat."

As they made their way to the barn, where they'd stabled Trail Blazer, he added, "I hope you didn't take offense when I laughed at some of the things Mr. Murdock said. I know how you feel about him and your grandmother, so I hope you don't think I was having fun at your expense. And I'm sorry if having me here made you uncomfortable."

"Actually, having you here made it easier. And to be honest, Elmer can be a real hoot at times." Amber shook her head, then blew out a sigh. "It's just that… well, besides the fact that I think they're so unsuited— and that Gram deserves someone better than him…"

"Someone more like your grandfather?"

Amber glanced up at Jensen, caught the look of compassion in his eyes, the understanding. "Yes, there's that, too. My grandfather was an amazing man, and I'm not ready for her to find a replacement. In fact, I doubt that I'll ever be ready for that."

Jensen slipped his hands into his pockets. "I know what you mean. I lost my father four years ago. He and my mother were soul mates, and I can't imagine her ever finding another man to take his place."

They stood like that for a moment, caught up in a shared moment—probably the only thing they really had in common. Then Jensen withdrew his pocket watch—a beautiful gold-embossed piece. She expected him to open it and check the time, yet he merely turned it over a time or two, then slipped it back into his pocket.

"Perhaps your grandmother is just enjoying a little camaraderie with Mr. Murdock and they've merely struck up a friendship of sorts."

"You may be right. And if that's all it is, I guess I shouldn't worry. But Elmer always has some fool wager going on. And I'm afraid she'll get hurt—emotionally, physically or even financially. Like I said, no good can possibly come from it."

Jensen stiffened. "If the man has a gambling problem, I can certainly see your concern."

"Well, it's not as though he's mortgaged his house or ran his credit into the ground. I think it's all penny-ante stuff. But he'd wager a nickel or a postage stamp or the button off his shirt, just to make things competitive. And Gram is so honest and straitlaced, she wouldn't take a shortcut home."

Jensen placed his index finger under Amber's chin in a move so sweet, so tender, that it should have been comforting—and it was—yet it stirred something in her blood, too. Something warm and sparkly.

"You're a good-hearted woman, Amber Rogers."

And…

She waited for what seemed to be the longest time for him to complete the thought—or maybe the connection he'd just made. But he did neither.

Doggone it.

But why would he? She and Jensen Fortune Chesterfield weren't any better suited than Helen Rogers and Elmer Murdock. And she was a fool to even let her thoughts drift in that direction. Because, like Gram and her silly crush, no good could come of it.

On the last day in December, while Quinn spent the afternoon at home with Amelia, Jensen took the opportunity to go for another ride on Trail Blazer.

He was still getting used to the stockier quarter horse breed and the Western tack. And while he was an exceptional horseman, he was adapting slowly.

As he cantered along on the spirited gelding, he pondered the possibility of purchasing a saddle of his own to keep in his brother-in-law's stable. In spite of his affinity for cowboy movies, he still preferred the English equestrian style for his own use.

He hadn't anticipated doing much riding at all when he'd flown to Texas for his sister's due date. But given the frequency of weddings and births taking place in America, he'd come to the realization that he would be most likely spending more time here in Horseback Hollow than he'd ever expected, so he didn't see it as a foolish investment.

After he rounded a large oak tree, he spotted a lone rider galloping toward him. He recognized the long blond hair flowing beneath the rim of the cowboy hat and watched as the cowgirl urged her mount forward.

Amber Rogers was quite the horsewoman, and Jensen pulled back on his reins, slowing so that he could fully enjoy the sight of her.

"Good morning," she said, as she pulled her horse alongside his.

"Hello, there. I thought I was still on Drummond land, but I must have crossed over onto your property line."

"Actually, this is neither. The county owns this area. It's full of riding trails, and if you follow this path far enough, you'll end up at the Hollow Springs Swimming Hole."

"A real swimming hole? Like that old movie with Marcia Mae Jones?"

At her confused look, he wondered whether Americans ever watched their own classic Western films.

But his excitement at seeing a true testament to the Wild West frontier couldn't be diminished.

"I would love to see it," he said. "How much farther do I need to ride?"

"About two miles. Come on." She turned her horse toward the narrow trail. "I'll take you up there."

He followed her slow pace and tried to keep his eyes on the trail and not her shapely bum. Thank goodness she wasn't riding at a quicker speed, otherwise he'd be completely useless ogling her graceful movements in the saddle.

When the trail widened and he pulled up alongside her, she said, "I didn't realize you were such an avid rider."

"Did you already have set expectations of me?"

"I really didn't know what to expect. The gossip magazines show you walking the red carpet and attending fabulous parties all over Europe. Of course, you're rarely smiling in those pictures, so I didn't know whether you disliked the photographers or if you're just one of those stoic Brits who doesn't know how to cut loose."

Did he really come across as that stuffy? Sure, he didn't always fancy the parties and the social commitments that came along with being a Fortune Chesterfield. But he smiled. Occasionally.

At least, he used to. Before his father's death. Yet, he didn't think mentioning this served any purpose. At the very least, it would put a damper on the present mood.

"Well, even the Brits know how to have fun," he said.

"And what, Mr. Jensen Fortune Chesterfield, do you do for fun?"

"I play polo. I attend the symphony. And I'm thinking about taking flying lessons." There he went with another reminder of his father. But instead of maintaining that painful topic, he changed the subject. "What do you do in your leisure time, Miss Amber Rogers—no relation to either Roy or to Rod?"

"I suppose you could say that I train and ride horses."

"From what I read online, you were one of the best barrel racers last year on the pro circuit."

"Oh, come now, you of all people know you shouldn't believe every news story you read." A flush of pink stole up her cheeks.

Was she embarrassed by her achievements? Or humbled by them? The tabloids had certainly exaggerated or downright lied about the things they often reported. But he assumed what he'd read about her was true.

"So then you haven't won several national titles?" he asked, wanting to hear more about her rodeo life.

"Not national titles. Just a few state ones. I was on track to go to the nationals in Las Vegas, but midseason, Pop passed away, and I left rodeoing to come back to the ranch and help Gram run things." Her eyes dimmed somewhat and took on a wistful gaze into the distance.

So he'd been right. She was being modest. From all accounts he'd read, she'd done very well in a short period of time and showed enough promise that the papers had expected her winning streak to continue. But she gave it all up rather quickly, and Jensen was learning the reason.

"Your grandparents raised you?" he asked.

"I was actually born in Lubbock, but my father died when I was five, and my mother and I moved in with his parents, Gram and Pop, after the funeral. Pop was a retired rodeo cowboy who bred and trained cutting horses. He was the one who trained me and encouraged me to follow my dream."

It sounded similar to Jensen's own father, who had encouraged him to play polo rather than follow family tradition and join the Royal Air Force. In fact, he and his father had been in the process of purchasing a polo

farm and investing in a couple of prize mares from
Argentina when Sir Simon died four years ago, taking
some of Jensen's dreams along with him.

"So you've put your future on hold to help run the
family business," he said.

"Pretty much. Besides the rodeo, I've never had
much of a plan for my life. I mean, it's not like Horseback Hollow is jumping with opportunities for barrel-
racing rodeo queens. I always figured I'd end up back
on the Broken R someday anyway, working with horses.
I suppose you can say that I just started doing that a bit
earlier than I expected."

Jensen nodded. "When my father passed away, it
forced me to step back and look at my life and what
I ought to be doing with it. Someone had to take over
the reins of the family investments and enterprises, as
well as Chesterfield Ltd., and since I'd been educated
and groomed to do so, I took the helm. Fortunately, I
can handle a lot of it remotely—although, with the time
difference, I'm working online and on Skype at some
strange hours."

"When do you sleep?" she asked.

"I find the time. I also take a nap now and then. The
most important thing to me has always been my family, and now that my father's gone, the responsibility
of looking after them has passed along to me. Hence
the reason I was so rude to you when you came to see
Amelia the other day. I fear I'm terribly overprotective."

Amber smiled. "I can understand that. I never had
any siblings. You're very lucky to have such a big family."

"I try to remind myself of that, although it does take
quite a bit of getting used to. As you may know, we only

recently met all of our Fortune cousins, so I'm still coming to terms with such a large addition to the family."

"But your British side of the family wasn't all that small."

No, it wasn't. His mother had been married before— to Rhys Henry Hayes. It hadn't been a happy union and had ended in divorce. The one good thing, though, was that it had produced Oliver and Brodie, Jensen's older brothers.

Fortunately, his mum had met Sir Simon, the love of her life, soon after. Together they'd had Jensen, followed by Charles, Lucie and Amelia.

"I suppose a family of six siblings sounds pretty large to an only child," he said.

"Large? I'd call it enormous. Do you get along?"

"Other than a few little tiffs now and again, yes. But I'd have to say we owe that to the parenting skills and the love of our mum and my father."

They rode through a tree-lined summit that opened up to a pristine and scenic waterfall. The red rock cliffs surrounding the swimming hole provided a stunning backdrop to the calm blue water below.

"Here it is. Horseback Hollow's hidden gem."

"I can see why the residents would want to keep it private. It's beautiful. Do you swim in it?" The thought of Amber Rogers in a two-piece swim costume stirred his blood in a way he hadn't expected.

"Not this time of year." She swung off her horse and tied the reins to a low-hanging branch of a nearby weeping willow tree. "But come summer, the place is hopping with kids and teenagers trying to beat the Texas heat. Personally, I like it best during the winter, when it's quiet and empty and a person can just ride up here and be all alone with their horse and their thoughts."

"Really? I wouldn't have pegged you for the quiet and introspective type." He regretted his word choice when she lifted a delicate brow at him.

"Do you picture me singing 'Happy Trails' around a campfire wearing fringes and a sequined hat like Dale Evans?"

"Maybe not singing, but I definitely can see you wearing fringes and sequins, riding faster than lightning through a cheering arena." He'd actually seen photographs of her when he'd looked her up on the internet.

Her shoulders slumped, and she gazed at the waterfall in the distance.

"I'm sorry," he said. "I didn't mean to hurt your feelings."

"No, it's not that. I guess I really do miss the rodeo life more than I expected. The glitz and the crowds are just a small part of my job. The practices and the injuries and hauling my horses and my gear all across the country was the hardest and biggest part, but all that work was worth it when the horn would sound, and I'd take off racing for that first barrel. I guess I should be lucky that I still get to work with horses and ride whenever I feel like it."

"But you still miss the excitement?"

"I really do. But I'm glad to be helping Gram, which, trust me, comes with its own share of excitement—as well as its confusion. I can't believe she'd even consider entering a dance contest. She never did anything like that with Pop. I didn't even know she *liked* to dance."

"Maybe she didn't know that until she met Mr. Murdock. My mother didn't know she'd come to love Texas barbecue until she came to Horseback Hollow for her first visit. Now, every time she flies back to England, she stuffs her luggage with jars of homemade rubs and sauces. A few months ago, she brought home a cooler filled with brisket and had our cook commission a company to install a smoker on the back lawn at our Chesterfield Estate."

Amber laughed, causing him to feel ten feet tall for bringing her out of her funk. "You're right. I'm sure you didn't realize how much you would love riding in that Western saddle."

"Oh no. You're wrong. As much as I like cowboy movies, and as hard as I've tried to adjust, I just can't seem to get used to this ghastly thing. I'm going into Lubbock later this week to custom order a proper English saddle. The pommel, the stirrups, everything just sits wrong on these American rigs."

"Really?" A mischievous glint flickered in her eyes. "Is that why you ride so slowly? Are you afraid you might lose your seating, fall out of that sturdy saddle and dirty those fancy white breeches?"

The corner of her mouth tilted. She was a cocky little thing—and in need of a lesson.

As Jensen strode to his horse, he wished he had one of his thoroughbreds back home for the challenge he was about to issue. "I'll wager I can ride faster than you, despite this inferior equestrian equipment my brother-in-law provided me."

"What do I get if I win?" she asked, already mounting up.

He thought for a moment, then grinned. "If I win, you fix me a proper English tea, complete with crumpets and clotted cream. If you win, I'll take you to a real-life authentic Texas barbecue joint." He adjusted the reins in his hands, knowing that the outcome of the bet was a win-win situation for him. Either way, he would get to spend more time with the lively and fun Amber Rogers.

"Well, Sir Jensen, I hope you like ribs, because next Monday night they have an all-you-can-eat special at my favorite spot in Vicker's Corners." With that parting comment, she took off.

He nudged Trail Blazer with his heels and leaned down over the gelding's neck, pretending he was racing for the polo ball with his mallet. Not only had he been team captain the last two years at university, but after graduation, he'd gone on to play competitively for England at the international level, so he had no doubt he could give her a good run. But after all the casseroles he'd been politely tolerating the past couple of weeks, he had a strong craving for some lighter fare—like some English cucumber sandwiches.

Still, in all honesty, some good ol' Texas barbecue wouldn't be bad, either. Especially in the company of a beautiful blonde cowgirl...

"How far are we going?" Amber called behind her, her hair whipping about her graceful neck.

"To that fork in the road where we met," he yelled back, trying to watch the trail and not her hips moving fluidly in the saddle.

When they finally reached the finish line, Amber was at least two lengths ahead of him. She pulled up first and slowed her horse to a walk as he did the same.

He hadn't enjoyed losing a race so much in his life.

They were both out of breath, but her shirt was the only one that had come unbuttoned at the top. He couldn't take his eyes off the way her breasts were heaving under the fitted plaid material.

He lifted his gaze long enough to see her smile. Maybe making the wager was a bad idea. Now he owed her dinner, yet he didn't know how he could sit across from her at a restaurant table and keep his thoughts strictly on the food.

"So when is dinner?" she asked.

"How about next Friday night? That way, we can avoid the New Year's holiday, as well as the all-you-can-eat crowd."

"That works for me."

"I'll pick you up at six."

"Sounds like a date," she said. "But under the circumstances, maybe it would be best if I met you there."

He pondered her suggestion for a moment longer than he probably should have because she added, "Don't you agree?"

And in truth? Probably so. No need to set the paparazzi to thinking there was another British royal enamored with a Horseback Hollow local. "You're right. Knowing the tabloids the way I do, they'd love to make something out of nothing."

"Well, they can't blame you for eating dinner with a neighbor."

"That's right."

"Oh, and please let Quinn know I'll be bringing Amelia's cutting horse over Friday." Then she turned in the direction of her ranch.

Jensen felt a bit like a heel when he and Trail Blazer headed in the opposite direction. He'd become adept at dealing with the tabloids. They printed blaring exaggerations about him all the time.

But the truth of the matter was, he didn't want Amber to get the wrong idea about them. He might be attracted to her, but that's as far as it would go.

So as they each headed home, the symbolism of them going their own ways at the fork in the road was both sad and true.

Bright and early Friday morning, on the second of January, Amber handpicked a filly she thought Amelia would like and brushed her until her coat shone. Then she loaded her in the trailer and drove her to the Drummond ranch.

Along the way, she spotted two cars parked on the side of the road, neither of which she recognized. She slowed up, mostly because she was going to turn, but also because curiosity niggled at her.

There seemed to be some whispering going on—a camera snatched out of one car and taken to another?

Uh-oh. Jensen had mentioned the media had tried all kinds of tricks, wanting to snap photos of a pregnant Amelia. She turned into the drive, yet continued to check her rearview mirror.

No cars...

Wait. A light blue sedan was parked in the shade of an oak tree. A man climbed out of the rear passenger seat. He was wearing black slacks and a white shirt. And he carried a camera with a huge telephoto lens.

The driver remained behind the wheel, but a second man got out, as well. And they proceeded to walk down the drive toward Quinn's house.

Nosy reporters.

Amber pulled up close to the barn and parked, but she left her purse in the truck. Then she marched up to the front door and knocked, prepared to tell Quinn or Amelia or whoever answered that there was possibly a cameraman and a reporter nearby.

Dang. Where was everyone? She knocked again.

Maybe they weren't home. Something told her they wouldn't like those reporters trespassing. Jensen had implied as much last Friday. But what should she do? Run the paparazzi off? Did she have a legal right to do that?

About the time she was going to walk away, the door swung open, and she looked up to see Jensen standing in the entryway.

"You came just in time for all the excitement," he said. "Just before dawn, my sister went into lab—"

"Jensen!" Amber had to shut him up. And there was only one way she could think of that would do so quickly. So she wrapped her arms around his neck and drew him into a close embrace, whispering, "There are a couple of reporters skulking around right behind me. Play along." Then she rose up on tiptoe and kissed him.

Chapter Four

Play along?

The moment Amber wrapped her arms around Jensen's neck and pressed her lips to his, it was easy to fall into the little scheme she'd concocted. His mouth was much too busy to speak, so he couldn't possibly blurt out that his sister had gone into labor. Nor could he tip off the reporter that Quinn had taken her to the hospital just a couple of hours ago, leaving Jensen the only one home on the ranch.

In fact, as Amber's peaches-and-cream scent enveloped him, as her lips parted and he tasted—brown sugar and…spice?—she leaned into him. He couldn't help but draw her close and caress the curve of her waist, the slope of her hips.

Who would have guessed such a feminine creature hid beneath all that denim and flannel?

And who would have known that the pretty cowgirl could kiss like this?

When the camera flashed behind them—not once, but a second time—Jensen came to his senses, ending the little sideshow they'd put on for the paparazzi. Amber may have saved his sister from being headline news, but she'd inadvertently given the tabloids another gossip-worthy story to publish. But he'd have to deal with that fallout later.

In the meantime, he took her by the hand and pulled her into the house—and out of the camera's view. Then he quickly shut the door behind them and turned to face her.

"I'm sorry," she said, "but I spotted a couple of men outside who had to be reporters. And I was afraid you were going to say something about Amelia being in labor, and I figured you wouldn't want them to hear that. So I did the only thing I could think of to shut you up."

She was quite flushed—not just her cheeks, which would explain a bit of embarrassment, but her throat and neck, too.

Had that kiss aroused more than gallantry on her part? It would seem so, and he couldn't help but smile.

"What's so funny?" she asked. "You were saying that Amelia was in something or other. And I jumped to the conclusion that she might be in labor."

"You're right. That's what I was going to say. And no, I didn't want the reporters to hear."

Amber brightened. "So Amelia really *is* in labor?"

"Yes, since early this morning. Quinn took her to the hospital in Lubbock right before dawn."

"So what are you doing? Waiting for a phone call?"

"That's exactly what I was doing. She wasn't due

until the first of next month, although her obstetrician didn't seem overly concerned. Still, I can't help worrying about it, though."

"I can understand that."

"She was under a great deal of stress early on, and those reporters made her life miserable. I can't help thinking that might have brought on early labor.

"But now they're outside again, ready to steal her joy and happiness again. They probably plan to camp out at the ranch until the baby's birth. Fortunately, she and Quinn managed to slip away while it was still dark, but now I'm undoubtedly stuck. I'm not sure how I'll go about leaving without them following me."

"Do you have the keys to that ranch pickup that's parked behind the barn?"

"Yes, the key should be hanging on the hook near the back door."

"Then maybe I can help. The reason I came was to bring that filly Quinn asked me to deliver. Why don't I go outside and make a big show of getting her out of the trailer? I can saddle her and do a little trick riding in the corral that's on the other side of the house. If the reporters are watching me, maybe you can slip out the back without them noticing you."

"How very Annie Oakley of you."

"Are you making fun of me?"

"On the contrary. I actually think it's quite a clever plan that just might work. And I do hope it does. Otherwise, I'll have to wait here and try to sneak out under the cloak of darkness."

"How very Sherlock Holmes of you."

He laughed. "What a team we make."

Now it was her turn to chuckle. "That's true. But just wait and see. We'll *git 'er done*, ol' chap."

"Apparently, we will. And those reporters won't know we've been having a go at their expense. Thanks for being my partner in crime."

"Anytime. That's the cowboy way." She glanced down at her scuffed boots, then back at him. "Hey. About that kiss…"

"Don't give it another thought, Amber."

She smiled, and the concern that had once troubled her brow eased. "Okay, then I won't."

He was glad that she seemed to shake it off as though it had never happened—the kiss and the reporters who'd recorded it all.

Unfortunately, he'd be thinking about it for the both of them—and not just the camera flash and the rippling effects of what that might mean. Because the memory of her taste, the feel of her in his arms, the flush on her cheeks and throat, would linger in his mind for a long, long time.

She'd jumped in to save the day, and it had worked in a surprising, blood-stirring way.

What an odd, mismatched team they made. The polo enthusiast and the cowgirl. The Brit and the Texan.

The tabloids were going to have a field day with that one.

Amber hadn't heard a word from Jensen or anyone remotely related to the Drummonds or the Fortunes since she'd run interference for them two days ago. And while she'd hoped someone would call to give her news about Amelia, she really hadn't expected them to.

She just hoped that everything went okay—and that the baby was healthy.

Other than her scattered thoughts, it had been business as usual on the Broken R. After breakfast, she'd lined up the foreman and ranch hands on the chores that needed to be done. Then she'd checked on the broodmares and worked with Lucky Charm, a gelding who was showing a lot of promise.

It had been a productive morning. That afternoon, Gram drove into town to run some errands and to pick up groceries at the Superette, while Amber went into the office and spent the next two hours paying bills, reconciling the checkbook and catching up on some year-end bookkeeping.

She'd no more than printed off a report for the accountant when the sound of an approaching vehicle caught her attention. She glanced out the window just in time to see Gram's Ford Taurus speed into the yard and skid to stop, a swirl of dust settling around the black sedan.

The mild-mannered woman never drove over the speed limit, and to come racing home...? Why, that bordered on recklessness.

See? Elmer Murdock *was* a bad influence on her.

Determined to ignore the behavior and not make any more fuss about Gram's dating habits, hoping that the excitement would run its course and fizzle out, Amber glanced down at the printout. That was, until Gram's shrill voice called out from the kitchen.

"Amber Sue Rogers! Get on out here as fast as your little legs will carry you. What in blue blazes is this all about?"

It had been ten or more years since Gram had lit

into Amber, although even then, she'd been fairly soft-spoken and mellow about it. So she was clearly worked up about something, and the angry shriek kicked Amber's pulse rate up a notch.

So after pushing back the desk chair, Amber hurried to the kitchen to see what all the commotion was about.

She found Gram standing beside the scarred oak table, holding a newspaper—or rather a tabloid—clucking her tongue and shaking her gray head.

"What's wrong?" Amber asked.

Gram turned the paper around and flashed a front page photo of a couple kissing. Well, not just any couple. It was Amber and Jensen standing smack-dab on Quinn Drummond's front porch.

Her heart thudded and rumbled like flat tire on a wheel that was falling off its axle.

How the heck did a national tabloid get a photo printed so quickly? Those dang reporters must have emailed it to the home office as soon as they took it, along with some cock-and-bull story to explain what they imagined they saw. Because other than the pictures they took of her riding the mare, there was nothing to report because she hadn't said a single word to them.

"Girl," Gram said, "you're front-page news. It doesn't list your name, but I know it's you. And so will everyone else in town."

Sure as shootin', it was Amber, all right. And there was no mistaking the headline, either. Sir Jensen and Texas Cowgirl Caught in Royal Liplock!

"What's this all about?" Gram asked.

"It wasn't a real kiss, if that's what you mean. And there's no romance going on between us. It was just an act, a ploy to distract a tabloid reporter who was hanging around the Drummond ranch."

"Distract him from what?"

"From learning that Amelia was in labor and that she'd been taken to the hospital."

Amber snatched the paper and scanned the article, which didn't appear to mention the Drummonds at all, other than to say that the Fortune Chesterfields seemed to be fixated on the "bucolic commoners in quaint Horseback Hollow."

What a crock of bull. They made normal, down-home country folk sound like a novelty that the rich and famous would soon grow tired of.

"Did the ploy work?" Gram asked.

Amber glanced up from her reading. "In terms of taking the heat off Amelia? Yes, it appears that way."

But now, it seemed that heat had been transferred on to Amber, who'd gotten her fifteen minutes of unwarranted and unwanted fame.

As she continued reading about how a brazen cowgirl had launched herself into Sir Jensen's arms in an attempt to rope a British royal…well, heck. She wanted to crawl into a hole and die.

Better yet, maybe she ought to rope herself a couple of reporters and hog-tie them until *they* wanted to crawl into a hole and die. It'd serve the nosy snoops right. She did have to admit, though, that the shots of her in the saddle were pretty good. She smiled, remembering the clicking of shutters and photographers' gasps as she nailed several of her trademark riding tricks. When it came to showmanship, she definitely had the knack.

"Speaking of Amelia," Gram said. "How is she? Did she have her baby?"

"I don't know." Amber set the tabloid on the table and tapped her finger at the photo that took up most of the front page. "After that silly kiss, I went outside and took the filly out of the trailer. Then I saddled her and proceeded to ride around the yard, doing a few tricks. If you turn the page, you'll see a couple of shots where I'm showing off for the cameraman and the reporter, which is how Jensen was able to slip away and head to the hospital."

Gram reached into the grocery bag, withdrew a tub of spreadable butter and placed it in the refrigerator. "I hope he appreciated your help because I'm afraid that article is going to make you look like a hussy."

Amber lifted her hand and fingered her lips, recalling the kiss that had shocked the wits out of Jensen—and had nearly stolen the breath out of her.

He seemed to have appreciated the diversion, although now she wasn't so sure. She might have just helped him exchange one sticky wicket for another.

The telephone rang, and Gram answered. "Hello? Yes, it is."

Amber didn't give the call much mind, thinking it was some kind of telemarketer or one of Gram's quilting friends wanting to be the first to know whether it was truly little tomboy Amber Rogers plastered all over the racks above the grocery store checkout aisles.

"Goodness, it's no bother at all. And yes, she's right here."

Her? As in *Amber*? Who could it possibly be? She didn't give people of any importance, like friends or someone from the casting department of Cowboy Country USA, the telephone number to the house. They called her cell. And speaking of that casting director—Perry or Terry What's-His-Name…

The guy had gotten it in his head that she could not only rope and ride, but that she'd look great dressed up as a saloon girl. So he'd been trying to talk her into auditioning for a part as a dance-hall girl in some indoor stage show they planned to have called Madame LaRue's Lone Star Review.

Never mind that Amber had never been to France and couldn't do the cancan. Apparently, they had dance instructors who could teach her all she needed to know.

"May I tell her who's calling?" Gram asked.

Boy, that guy was sure persistent.

"Why, hello, Jensen. I'll get her." Gram covered the telephone receiver and whispered, "I knew it was him, but I didn't want him to think I was all gaga over him like some folks in town—especially after that stupid tabloid hit the newsstand."

She was right. Some of the locals saw dollar signs whenever they spotted one of the Fortunes because they considered them as rich as ol' fury. And with the Fortune Chesterfields now in town, some people acted as though they were related to the queen of England.

Amber took the receiver, cleared her throat and willed her voice to sound as though kissing royalty and being on the front page of a tabloid were just as normal as…well as wearing a saloon-girl costume and dancing the cancan.

"Hey," she said. "I'm glad you called, Jensen. How's your sister? Did she have the baby?"

"She's doing splendidly. She had a beautiful baby girl early this morning—about six o'clock."

She was in labor for two days? "It sounds as though she had a rough time of it."

"Actually, her labor would start, then stop. And because she wasn't due until the first of February, her doctor was reluctant to induce her labor—or to send her home. She wasn't overly uncomfortable until last night, when her water broke—and then they gave her an epidural."

"How much did the baby weigh?"

"2.7 kilograms."

Amber's breath caught. "That sounds awfully small. Is everything okay?"

He paused. "Oh, I'm sorry. I forgot that you Americans aren't on the metric system. She weighs about six pounds—maybe a bit less."

"Then she wasn't too small. You Brits do things so differently."

"I'm afraid it's the other way around, my dear. But I'm much too happy to argue with you. Mother and daughter are doing very well."

"I'm glad to hear it." Amber blew out a sigh of relief. "I'd been wondering how things were going—and I'd planned to call Jeanne Marie and ask."

"You would have had to call her on the mobile. She's here at the hospital with us."

"That's not surprising. I'm sure she's been nearly as excited about the new baby as your mother is."

"That's true. They're both beside themselves and planning shopping trips already—now that they know the baby is a girl." Jensen laughed.

"Well, thanks for calling," Amber said.

"I also wanted to let you know that Amelia would like to speak with you."

Amber glanced at the tabloid on the kitchen table. No doubt Jensen's sister had gotten wind of the latest gossip. The realization poked at her like a pinprick to a helium balloon, and all the levity she'd experienced a heartbeat ago whooshed out, leaving her empty, deflated.

Was the new mother upset about her providing more Chesterfield fodder for the news rags? Had it caused her more grief and uneasiness on a day that should have been one of the happiest of her life?

Maybe Amelia wanted to ask Amber to stay away from her, Quinn and the baby from now on.

If that was the case, this would be her first—and maybe her only chance—to see the baby. At least, until Jensen left town and news of the poor and desperate cowgirl's attempts to land a royal husband died down.

"Can you slip away for a while?" Jensen asked. "The nursing staff have strict orders not to allow any visitors, other than the ones who are already here and are now leaving, but I can get you in."

"Amelia wants to see me in person? *Today?*"

Couldn't it wait until she was released from the hospital? Until she was feeling better?

"Yes," Jensen said. "So I thought it might be best if you met me someplace discreet."

No doubt because the reporters hadn't shown up at the hospital yet. And since they probably assumed Amelia and Quinn were still at the ranch. Maybe they were staked out there, so Jensen was afraid to go home. Or maybe they were now following Amber.

"Sure," she said. "Of course. Where do you think we should meet?"

"I know this sounds pretty clandestine, but if your

grandmother wouldn't mind driving you into town later this evening, she could drop you off at one of the local eateries. Then maybe you could slip out the back door, and I could pick you up."

"Perhaps I should wear a costume of some kind."

"I don't know if that would be completely necessary."

Amber had meant the comment to be tongue-in-cheek, but Jensen clearly hadn't picked up on it. So she took it a step further. "A black trench coat might be better than cutting eyeholes out of a brown paper bag and wearing it over my head."

"Are you annoyed?" he asked.

"Mostly with myself and this darned predicament I seem to have gotten us into. I should have known better than to have kissed you."

Silence stretched across the telephone line for a moment, and she was suddenly more embarrassed about bringing up the kiss rather than the entire incident itself. And why was that?

"For the record," he said, "I thought that kiss was rather nice."

"Nice? Well, that's a relief. At least you didn't find it dull or nasty."

"In spite of what you said to the contrary, it appears that I've managed to offend you yet again and that was never my intention."

Amber blew out a sigh. "I'm sorry, Jensen. It's just that I'm looking at a blasted tabloid and reading about how I've set my sights on marrying a British prince so I can move to London and drink tea with the queen. And all I was trying to do was help you and your family. Now people are going to think I'm some kind of highfalutin gold digger."

"I know better than that. And I would wager that most people who know you would agree."

A slow smile stretched across her face. "Thank you for that. I just hope your sister and the rest of your family does, too."

"We're aware of how the paparazzi creates stories out of nothing. This is old hat for us. So don't worry about anyone from my family believing that rot."

She supposed that was true. But his sister was trying to live a normal life in Horseback Hollow, and she probably didn't care for any extra notoriety these days.

Still, Amber couldn't imagine why Amelia would want to speak to her, especially now—and in person. It couldn't possibly be about anything other than the media headlines. And to be honest, Amber dreaded the meeting.

But she wasn't a coward. So she'd have to face the music—or in this case, the new mama.

In spite of Jensen's assurance that they act normally, it still seemed pretty cloak-and-dagger to Amber.

At exactly seven o'clock, she and Gram pulled into the parking lot of the VFW, where they left the Ford Taurus next to Elmer Murdock's army-green Dodge Charger. Amber wore her customary Wrangler jeans, although she'd chosen a white feminine blouse and a new black sweater to ward off the winter chill. She'd also applied more makeup than usual and had left her hair long and loose, the tendrils glossy and curled on the ends.

Then she and Gram went inside to meet her grandmother's unlikely gentleman friend. Amber stayed long enough to drink a diet soda, to make small talk and to ask Elmer to drive Gram back to the ranch. Needless to say, the Korean War vet was more than happy to oblige—and Gram was pleased with the game plan, too.

Twenty minutes later, as dusk was settling over Horseback Hollow, Amber excused herself and walked to the feed store, which was closed. But that didn't matter. She had no intention of going inside. Instead, she slipped around to the back, where Jensen was waiting for her in Quinn's pickup, the engine idling. Then she opened the passenger door, climbed inside and off they went.

They traveled a circuitous route to the hospital in Lubbock, arriving well after dark—and right before visiting hours ended for the night.

As they entered the lobby, which still bore Christmas decorations although New Year's had just passed, Amber said, "It looks like we managed to avoid those pesky reporters."

"This time, and when you outwitted them two days ago and helped me escaped. You're a clever actress. Your ploy worked."

Jensen probably had no idea how his compliment pleased her, how it pumped her confidence and encouraged her to go ahead and audition for Madame LaRue's Lone Star Review. Why not? It might be fun, whether she landed the spot or not.

When they stopped at the elevator, he pushed the up button, then turned to her and smiled. "Perhaps you should be living in Hollywood instead of Horseback Hollow."

Fortunately for her, with Cowboy Country USA opening just outside town, she wouldn't have to move from the ranch at all. "Thanks. Play-acting is a tal-

ent I'm just learning to perfect." And just in case he'd
read too much into that little kiss she'd given him, she
added, "So don't get too caught up in the local gossip
about me being swept off my boots by you. That little
smooch was all part of the show."

"Is that right?" His lips quirked into a sly grin.

He might be having fun at her expense, but she ig-
nored the tease and merely nodded.

"Then you really are a jolly good actress." He
reached out and fingered her throat, where her pulse
fluttered. Dang. Did he feel it trembling?

She swallowed, no doubt giving him something else
to feel in there.

Where the heck was that darn elevator?

But she shook off the pesky little flutters and trem-
bles. "What are you getting at?"

"That kiss on Quinn's porch. The one you said was
no big deal."

"What about it?"

"Afterward, when we went inside, your cheeks were
rosy. But so was your neck and throat. How did you
manage to get that flush to spread like that? I'm amazed
that you were able to just close your eyes and conjure it
there with no help from me or any good, old-fashioned
chemistry. Like I said, you're a very good actress. Either that, or a very bad liar."

She had to admit she'd been shaken by the kiss, although she hadn't wanted to admit it to him—or even
to herself.

But the trouble was, she had been thinking about it a
lot more than she should. It may have started out as an
act—all fun and games. But she'd never experienced a

kiss quite like that before and she doubted she'd ever experience the like again.

Fortunately, the elevator door finally opened, interrupting the intense questioning of his eyes and allowing her to pretend as though they'd been talking about something else.

"All aboard," she said. "Which floor is Amelia on?"

"The fourth."

Before she could push the button, two other people joined them. *Thank goodness! Saved by strangers.*

A couple of elevator dings later, Jensen walked Amber through the double doors that led to the maternity ward and on to room 411, where they found Amelia comfortably nestled in her hospital bed, holding her daughter in her arms.

The tired but glowing new mother looked up from the precious swaddled bundle. "Oh, good. You're here. Thank you for coming, Amber."

"Where is everyone?" Jensen asked.

"Mum and Aunt Jeanne Marie just left with Quinn. They're having dinner at a restaurant down the street. I believe they'll be heading back to Horseback Hollow, but Quinn will be staying the night with the baby and me. And he promised to bring me back some shepherd's pie. I don't know when these pregnancy cravings will go away, but this hospital food isn't really to my liking."

Amanda eased closer to the bed and peered at the sweet newborn who dozed in her mother's arms. "She's beautiful. And so small. But I'm sure she'll be playing dress up with her cousin Piper and pushing dollies in their strollers in no time at all."

"I'm sure you're right. Plus, Quinn's sister Jess just

gave birth to a baby girl two nights ago. So she has another new cousin to play with."

"Three little girls all close in age," Amber said. "Won't that be fun?"

"What's especially nice is that Jess and Mac have five sons so, needless to say, they're delighted to finally have a daughter to love and spoil."

"I'll bet they are!"

As Amber and Amelia marveled over the sweet newborn, Jensen asked his sister, "Is there anything you need? I'd be happy to pick it up for you."

"I talked to Stacey," Amelia said, "and I think I'm going to need more nappies."

"I'm sure you will," Amber said. "From what I hear, newborns don't sleep through the night for several months. So you won't be getting much sleep."

Jensen furrowed his brow. "What does sleep have to do with it?"

"Taking naps?" Amber asked. "I would think that your sister will need to take plenty of them."

Amelia laughed. "I was talking about diapers. We call them nappies in England."

"You've sure done some strange things with our language," Amber said.

Jensen gave her a little nudge. "I beg to differ. If I remember my history lessons, the English language was well established before your little American colony began butchering it."

Amber elbowed him right back. "And we dumped your tea into the harbor and taught you a lesson or two, if I remember correctly."

"Listen, you two, if your revolution reenactment wakes the baby, I'll have to ask you to take it outside my hospital room," Amelia said, as she smirked and nuzzled her newborn closer.

"We'll save it for later," Jensen said. "Besides, visiting hours are nearly over."

"Then, if you don't mind, I'd like to talk to Amber alone."

"Of course," Jensen said. "I'll step outside into the hallway."

Here it comes. Amelia was going to lay into her for practically mauling her brother in public. But Amber was a big girl. She could take her licking.

"Thank you for distracting that reporter at the ranch," Amelia said. "It allowed Quinn and I to have our privacy during this special time in our lives."

"You're welcome. Although, I apologize for opening up a whole new can of worms for those crazy tabloids. Now they think Jensen and I are a hot topic."

"Would that be so bad?"

Amber drew back. Was she kidding? While a lot of mothers opted for natural childbirth, the British woman must've chosen to use drugs. Was Amelia flying high on some kind of medicine that bypassed her baby's bloodstream but had her dreaming romantic fantasies?

Amelia studied Amber carefully, smiled and nodded. "You're just what Jensen needs."

Seriously? Amber slowly shook her head. "I'm afraid you've got it all wrong. It was just a little kiss between friends."

"The camera caught a spark. And I've seen the banter between you. My brother hasn't lit up like that since before my father passed away. And even then...well, I think there's something going on."

Oh, boy. Maybe the euphoria of being a new mother

was making her see things that clearly weren't there. "I'm afraid it was all an act."

Amelia shook her head. "You can deny your feelings the way I denied mine for Quinn. But it will be futile. Once my brother sets his sights on a prime piece of horseflesh, he can be as stubborn as Churchill's bulldog."

Had Amelia just called her a horse?

The Brits had such an odd way with words. Maybe it was best that Amber not take offense, especially when the new mother had been so sweet and so understanding.

Amelia glanced down at her little one, then checked the baby's diaper. "Well, what do you know? I'm going to have to change her nappy, then put her down for a nappy."

They both laughed.

"I'll let you get to it, then," Amber said. "And it's probably a good idea if you both get some rest. Thanks so much for understanding about that darn photo." Even if Amelia didn't understand that nothing was going on between Amber and her brother.

"Thank you. We might need you to pull another stunt to help us sneak home undetected."

"I don't know about that. I'm afraid this cowgirl isn't used to being front-page news. But I'll run the idea past Jensen." She tossed her new friend a smile. "You have a beautiful baby, Amelia. Take care."

Then she slipped out of the room and went in search of Jensen. She found him near the water fountain in the corridor.

"That was quick," he said. "What did she have to say?"

"Not much. She thanked me for helping lead the paparazzi astray. That kind of thing."

As they continued out of the hospital, he glanced her way a couple of times. She figured he wasn't buying her explanation. But there was no way she'd tell him what Amelia had really said, especially about there being some kind of spark in that kiss—as nice and moving as it was. Or that he needed someone like Amber. Imagine that.

He opened the lobby door, and they stepped out into the winter night.

"I forgot to ask if they'd chosen a name for the baby." In truth, she'd been so worried about the conversation Amelia intended to have with her that she'd been thrown off step.

"Clementine Rose."

"How cool is that? Your sister gave her daughter a Western name."

"What do you mean?"

Amber broke into song, singing the familiar old diddy that Pop used to hum all the time, "Oh, my darlin', oh, my darlin', oh my darlin', Clementine…"

"Actually," Jensen said, "the baby was named after my father's mother—Clementine."

"Oh. And the Rose…?"

"Amelia just likes the name."

Jensen opened the passenger door of Quinn's pickup, and Amber slid inside. Then he climbed behind the wheel and they were off.

The ride back to Horseback Hollow was pretty quiet, the silence stretching between them like a taut rubber band that was ready to snap.

When they finally reached the feed store, where

they'd met earlier, he parked in front, under an old streetlight that wasn't working. It was only a couple of doors down from the VFW, where Gram had left the Taurus for Amber to drive home.

When Amber reached for the door handle, Jensen asked, "What's really bothering you?"

She turned back, deciding to finally level with him. But instead of taking her time to think up a careful explanation, her words came out in a near rush after being pent up for so dang long. "It's just that Amelia thinks we're really a couple, and I know that's not true. Heck, we're barely even friends. Anyone can see that. A man like you would never want a girl like me, and you're probably laughing on the inside and—"

Jensen leaned across the seat, placed a hand behind her neck, drew her lips to his and stopped her deluge of words with a kiss that soon deepened to the point that her hands didn't want to stay put.

Amber wasn't sure how long it would have lasted or what it might have led to if Jensen hadn't inadvertently leaned against the horn, setting off a loud, earsplitting honk that made them jerk apart and left them both breathless.

"What...was...that...kiss?" She stopped, her words coming out in raspy little gasps.

"...all about?" he finished for her.

She merely nodded.

"I don't know. It just seemed like an easier thing to do than to discuss."

Maybe so, but being with Jensen was still pretty clandestine, what with meeting in the shadows, under the cloak of darkness.

The British royal and the cowgirl. They might be attracted to each other—and she might be good enough for him to entertain the idea of a few kisses in private or even a brief, heated affair. And maybe she ought to consider the same thing for herself, too.

But it would never last. Especially if the press—or the town gossips—got wind of it.

So she shook it all off—the secretive nature of it all, as well as the sparks and the chemistry, and opened the passenger door. "Good night, Jensen."

"What about dinner?" he asked. "I still owe you, remember?"

Yep, she remembered. Trouble was, she was afraid if she got in any deeper with him, there'd be a lot she'd have a hard time forgetting.

"We'll talk about it later," she said.

"Tomorrow?"

"Sure. Why not?"

"I may have to take my brother and sister to the airport, although I'm not sure when. I'll have to find out. Maybe we can set something up after I get home."

"Maybe so." She wasn't going to count on it, though. Especially when she had the feeling he wouldn't want to be seen out in public with her—where the newshounds or local gossips might spot them.

But as she headed for her car, she wondered if, when he set his mind on something, he might be as persistent as those pesky reporters he tried to avoid.

Well, Amber Rogers was no pushover. And if Jensen Fortune Chesterfield thought he'd met someone different from his usual fare—he didn't know the half of it. Because he'd more than met his match.

Chapter Five

Jensen wasn't surprised that his younger sister and brother wanted to return to London as soon as Amelia came home from the hospital with baby Clementine Rose. He'd briefly contemplated flying back with them, then returning for the weddings next month. But his mother wanted him to stay awhile longer, and he'd agreed for more reasons than one.

He'd broken things off with Monica Wainwright just before the holidays, so the trip to America had allowed him to put some distance between them.

The early days of their short-lived romance had been somewhat pleasant, but then she'd let down her guard and had shown him a selfish and haughty side he couldn't tolerate.

Besides, he owed Amber dinner for that horse race he'd lost, something he was actually looking forward to. But as soon as the weddings were over in February, he'd be making this trip to the airfield himself, rather than driving his two younger siblings and dropping them off.

So, with the flight plan set, Jensen waited for Quinn to retrieve the car keys.

"Here you go," the proud new father said.

"Thank you. It won't take long."

"It doesn't matter. Keep the car as long as you want."

Lady Josephine, who'd just entered the living room from the kitchen, said, "Wait for me, Jensen. I'd like to ride with you."

"You don't need to do that, Mum. I'm sure Charles and Lucie will understand if you'd rather stay here with baby Clementine."

"Yes, I know, but Quinn and Amelia would probably like some time to themselves, and I'd enjoy an outing. It also gives me a chance to see Sawyer and Laurel. I haven't talked to my brother's son or his wife since Christmas. Just let me freshen my makeup. I'll meet you in the car."

A few minutes later, Lady Josephine had not only applied a fresh coat of lipstick and face powder, but a subtle touch of Chanel No. 5. After she slid into the passenger seat, Jensen drove them to the B and B in Vicker's Corners, where Charles and Lucie had been staying.

Just as he'd suspected, his younger brother and sister were waiting in front of the quaint, three-story building with its green-and-white striped awnings. After they loaded the luggage in the car, they headed to the small airfield.

As Jensen turned onto the country road that led to the small terminal, his mother glanced over her shoulder and into the backseat, where Lucie and Charles sat. "Be sure to check on Oliver and ask about Ollie. I miss that little boy so. And let me know if there is anything I should be concerned about."

Oliver, their oldest half brother, had divorced last year. His toddler son lived with his ex-wife.

"We'll do that," Charles said. "But I'm sure Oliver would let you know if there was anything to worry about."

Jensen wasn't so sure about that. He wasn't the only one who didn't like to see their mother overly concerned about things she had no control over.

"But, Mum," Charles asked, "can Lucie and I trust you to take care of baby Clemmie for us?"

At that ridiculous notion, laughter erupted. Even Lady Josephine smiled at her youngest son's attempt to lighten the mood.

She was still grinning from ear to ear when Jensen parked in front of Redmond-Fortune Air, the flight school and charter service owned by Sawyer Fortune and his wife, Laurel.

The new building they'd built last year, with its gray block walls, smoky glass windows and chrome trim, had modernized the small airport, which up until that point had only amounted to a small control tower, a couple of modular buildings, several hangars and the airstrip.

Jensen had no more than shut off the engine when Josephine exited the car and was heading for the entrance.

How strange. But then again, Mum had mentioned that she was eager to see Sawyer and Laurel.

Lucie trailed their mother while Jensen and Charles brought up the rear, carrying the luggage.

The small reception area was empty, although Orlando Mendoza, one of the pilots, sat in a chair, holding his smartphone and sending a text.

Upon seeing Lady Josephine, the handsome man with graying hair and sun-bronzed skin broke into a smile then stood and took her hand. "Good afternoon. What a pleasure to see you."

She flushed. "Will you be flying Charles and Lucie to Dallas?"

"No, I'm afraid not," Orlando said. "I had an early day. I just completed a charter flight to Houston, so I'm heading home. At least, I will be as soon as Sawyer returns." Orlando glanced out the window toward the parking lot, then back to Jensen. "I don't suppose you happen to be heading back through town?"

"No, but it's not too far out of the way. Why?"

"I had car trouble this morning, and my nephew, Marcos, gave me a ride to work."

Marcos Mendoza and his wife Wendy owned the Hollows Cantina.

"I'd be happy to drop you off," Jensen told Orlando.

"Are you sure it won't be any trouble?"

"Not at all."

While Orlando made small talk with his mother and siblings, Jensen wandered off to look at a table that held a plastic-enclosed display of miniature-sized scale-model aircraft. As he did so, he reached into his pocket and felt the gold watch that rested there.

He and his father used to stop by the small airfield near the Chesterfield estate, where they would watch the planes take off and land. It had been a special time, when they talked about life and hopes and dreams. Not a plane flew overhead without Jensen remembering those days.

A door swung open, and he turned to see Laurel Redmond Fortune enter the reception area of the terminal. The lovely blonde pilot had once flown jets for the United States Air Force.

After greeting Josephine and then Lucie with a warm embrace, Laurel shook hands with Charles, who could be rather stuffy at times.

"I'll be flying you to Dallas today," Laurel said. "Are you ready to go?"

Charles reached for his bags. "We certainly are. We've had a lovely time, but Lucie and I are eager to get home."

"Hey." Laurel glanced at Jensen, who stood off to the side—no doubt appearing to be as stuffy as Charles and, perhaps, more distant. "I don't suppose you're heading back into town after this?"

Jensen left the miniature airplanes, as well as his musing behind. "Orlando mentioned he needed a ride, so I'll take him wherever he wants to go."

Laurel gave him a thumbs-up, then walked out the door to the airfield, with Lucie and Charles on her heels, each carrying their own bags.

"Marcos promised to have someone fix my car while I was gone," Orlando said. "So, if you don't mind dropping me off at the Hollows Cantina, that would be perfect."

"Splendid," Josephine said. "Jensen and I haven't eaten yet, and I've had a craving for a crock of their crab dip and those tasty rice crackers."

What? No hurry to get back home to the new grandbaby? Apparently, his mum really did want the new parents to bond.

"Great," Orlando said. "I'll buy you a margarita for your trouble."

Jensen was just about to tell him that wouldn't be necessary when his mum blushed and patted the pilot's arm. "That would be lovely, Orlando."

Since when had she switched from wine to margaritas? Interestingly, Texas was beginning to have an odd effect on her.

Yet wasn't it having an odd effect on Jensen, too?

Horseback Hollow certainly didn't have a drop of culture, nor did it offer any of the nightlife he enjoyed in London. Yet he found the quaint Western town appealing—from a tourist's standpoint, of course.

He was far more comfortable on his country estate and playing polo at the nicest clubs in the UK, but he'd make the best of it for the month or so that he'd be here. Which meant spending more time with Amber Rogers.

Should he call her and ask her to meet him at the Hollows Cantina? Maybe not. But to be perfectly honest, at least with himself, he wouldn't mind sharing another kiss with her—or possibly even more than that.

Amber's stomach had been growling all throughout her Wild West Show tryout and, as she'd pulled up to the Hollows Cantina, she thought her belly would soon be ordering for her. Less than an hour ago, she'd delivered a performance that would've really knocked the socks off those so-called journalists who'd been camped out around the Drummond property.

She put the old truck in Park and checked the trailer she'd been towing to ensure that Danny Boy was resting comfortably after the barrel racing display he'd helped her put on earlier today. When she'd sat down with the bigwigs at Cowboy Country USA afterward, she let them know that if they signed her as one of their lead acts, she'd only use her own horses.

The executives had made her a surprisingly good offer, and she'd promised to have her attorney look over the contract and get back to them within a week.

She gave Danny Boy a pat and promised him a treat after dinner. Then she hitched her purse higher on her shoulder and headed into the restaurant, which was sure hopping tonight.

It was a cool place to gather, but it had gotten some flack from the locals who considered it a "rich folks' establishment" and feared that it would ruin the small town's ambiance.

The same people were against Cowboy Country USA, although their number appeared to have doubled as more of the locals jumped on the bandwagon to complain about the theme park. Even Deke and Jeanne Marie hadn't kept their objections secret. And from what Amber had gathered, most of their kids agreed.

Still, Marcos and Wendy Mendoza were seeing an increase in business these days, thanks to the Cowboy Country bigwigs frequenting the Hollows Cantina and holding some of their meetings here. So she suspected they weren't opposed to the theme park, although they were smart enough to keep their opinions to themselves.

Once inside the busy restaurant, she was met by the hostess, Rachel Robinson, who was new in town and resembled a less-glamorous Angelina Jolie.

Rachel flashed a bright-eyed smile. "Good evening, Amber. We're pretty full tonight. You're looking at a fifteen-to-twenty-minute wait unless you want to sit upstairs."

"I'm meeting my grandmother for dinner, and since things get a little chilly and loud up there, I think we'd better wait for a table down here—hopefully in a quiet, out-of-the-way spot."

"Mrs. Rogers is already here with Mr. Murdock," Rachel said. "They mentioned that someone would be joining them. I didn't realize it would be you. And they're seated upstairs."

How do you like that? Elmer Murdock was a party crasher.

"I can show you where they are," Rachel said.

"That's okay. I'll find them." Amber made her way to the middle of the room and climbed the staircase with wide iron railings and rustic wooden steps to the second floor.

She'd no more than reached the landing when she spotted Gram's trademark French twist at a table near the dance floor. Normally her grandmother kept to the quiet corners of any location, but the place was so packed, they must have seated her in the only available spot.

Amber made her way to the table and greeted her grandmother with a kiss on the cheek, just as a huge margarita glass was thrust in front of her.

No, make that *two* huge margarita glasses, each with a shot glass filled with tequila attached to the side.

And the server was none other than Elmer Murdock. "Two of the cantina's finest drinks for two of the finest women in the joint."

Gram smiled up at the man. "Why, thank you, Elmer."

Apparently, the retired marine was too busy to notice Gram's appreciation since he was asking the server, who was carrying his beer, to bring over a salt shaker and some limes.

What was he doing here? And why was he under the impression that Gram would be throwing back margaritas and shots of Jose Cuervo like a coed on spring break?

The uninvited bearer of alcoholic beverages pulled out a seat and sat a little closer to Gram than was entirely necessary, given they were at a table for four.

If he noticed Amber's lack of enthusiasm, it didn't seem to bother him. "Drink up, gals. It's a twofer one special, and we got another thirty minutes before happy hour is over."

Amber had barely registered the cheapskate comment before Elmer threw her for the next loop of the evening. "So, girlie, how did the big audition go?"

"Shhh!" Amber hoped he'd lower his voice, but she was afraid she'd have better luck trying to get a stampede of wild broncs to jump through a Hula-Hoop.

"Why?" he asked. "You ought to be pleased as punch that they'd come after you like they're doing. They know a class act when they see one."

What in blue blazes did someone like Gram, who was so refined and quiet, see in such a loudmouthed character like Elmer Murdock?

Amber took a gulp of the margarita and decided the quick hit of liquid calm would be worth the brain freeze she'd get from downing the cold drink so quickly.

Fortunately, Gram came to her rescue. "Elmer, dear, Amber wasn't quite ready to tell anyone about—"

Amber gave a discreet cough.

"Whoops." Elmer took a sip of his beer and reached into the communal basket of chips. "I won't say another word about it, then. Old Elmer Murdock is like a vault. You wouldn't believe all the secrets I know."

That was a relief. And if she took the job at Cowboy Country USA, which she planned to do, everyone would find out anyway. The lines were already being drawn in the town sand since many of the locals weren't exactly giving a warm Texas welcome to the Wild West theme park, and she'd soon be grist for the gossip mill.

She took another sip of the sweet-and-sour drink, this time a little slower than the first. She scanned the restaurant, trying to see who might have overheard the comment made by Gram's third wheel.

Of course, from the way Elmer was showing her grandmother how to lick the salt and then squeeze the lime after drinking down her tequila, Amber would have to assume that *she* was the third wheel.

"Miss Rogers! I'm so glad you're here."

Amber glanced up to see Perry—or was it Terry?—from the Cowboy Country casting department.

He must have noticed her befuddled look because he reached out his hand and said, "Larry Byerly. Cowboy Country USA."

She knew who he was. They'd met before and talked on the phone several times. It was merely his first name she was having trouble with. But she let it go at that and shook his hand.

"After that little performance you put on today down at the county fairgrounds, news traveled like wildfire. And I was told to sign that girl come hell or high water."

She'd already agreed to sign with the Wild West Show if her attorney didn't see a problem with the contract, so news didn't travel nearly as fast as Larry thought it did.

"What can I do for you?" she asked.

"It's what *I* can do for *you*. If I could just have a minute or two to speak with you in private—that's really all I need. The PR department is chomping at the bit to get a pretty local girl to feature in our ads and quite possibly the Lone Star Review. And Miss Rogers, we're all convinced that gal is you."

Again, Amber scanned the room. Luckily, there wasn't anyone around who seemed to be paying attention—other than Gram and Elmer, who were leaning into the conversation as though the fate of the entire world rested on Amber's answer. Or at least, life as they knew it in Horseback Hollow, which was crazy.

The only one she was really concerned about seeing her talk to the enemy, so to speak, was Jensen. But why stress about that?

The Hollows Cantina might be the nicest restaurant in town, but it wouldn't be Jensen's cup of tea. Besides, what did he care what she did with her life or her future anyway?

The Hollows Cantina was busy tonight. Each of the outdoor tables that lined the sidewalk was taken, the heaters blasting to keep the bundled-up diners protected from the brisk, January evening.

The second story, an open-air terrace adorned with little white lights, appeared to be just as full.

Jensen opened the door for his mother, and she stepped inside, followed by Orlando.

The distinguished pilot greeted the hostess, a lovely brunette with long straight hair and striking blue eyes. "Looks like you have a full house tonight, Rachel."

"We do, but I have a table upstairs. It's not quite

ready. If you don't mind waiting a couple of minutes, I'll take you to it."

"That's fine," Jensen said. "Thank you."

"You were telling me about your sons," Josephine said to Orlando.

"Yes, Cisco and Matteo have just settled in Horseback Hollow. I'm glad to have them nearby."

"I'm sure you are. I'll be spending more time here, now that..." She scanned the area, then lowered her voice. "Well, you know."

Orlando nodded. "I completely understand. Maybe you should consider getting a small home here, unless you want to stay with your daughter and son-in-law."

"That's a good idea, Orlando. I'll give that some thought. Maybe I can encourage my other children to buy vacation homes in Horseback Hollow. I think it would be especially good for Oliver and Brodie to have a closer relationship with their new family—at least for part of the year."

Jensen couldn't imagine either of his older brothers leaving the UK. Goodness, even Charles and Lucie couldn't get home fast enough as it was.

"Your table is ready," the hostess—Rachel—said. Then the attractive woman led them upstairs.

Jensen had no more than reached the landing when he spotted Amber seated at a table near the bar with a man he didn't recognize.

The gent was older than she—in his forties perhaps. Not bad looking—if you liked men who wore golf clothing when they socialized.

"Is this table all right?" the hostess asked, drawing Jensen's attention, but just barely.

"It's fine. Thank you."

Orlando held a chair for Josephine, yet Jensen couldn't seem to take a seat. His interest was drawn to that table for two, especially because the older man leaned forward as though pressing Amber, urging her to…?

What?

"Is there something wrong, sir?" the hostess asked.

Jensen snapped his attention back to the people he was with. "No, I'm sorry. I thought I spotted someone I knew."

His mum chuckled softly. "You did, son. Isn't that Amber Rogers, the young woman who owns the ranch near Quinn's?"

"Um. Yes," he said. "So it is."

"If I'm not mistaken, that also appears to be the young woman the tabloids spotted with you…perhaps… Photoshopped a perfectly simple picture to look like the two of you were kissing."

Jensen reached for a glass of water and took a sip. He knew exactly where this conversation was heading, and he wished she'd let it drop—especially in front of Orlando.

"I wonder who that man is?" his mother asked. "He seems quite enamored of Amber. But then, what man wouldn't be. She's actually quite lovely."

Jensen ought to be annoyed with his mum for taunting him, but he was too caught up in what was going on at Amber's table. He couldn't help his interest—nor the sharp poke of jealousy that needled him.

Somewhere along the way, they'd placed drink orders, and he'd ended up with a longneck bottle of beer. But he couldn't seem to focus on anything but Amber and that older man who was doing all the talking.

What in the hell was he saying?

She actually looked as though she'd rather be somewhere else.

Did she want to escape? Jensen was feeling rather chivalrous.

His mother was saying something, although he'd be damned if he knew what it was. He'd completely lost track of the conversation at his table and decided to put an end to his curiosity.

So he picked up his bottle of beer, stood and said the only two words he'd wanted to say since laying eyes on Amber just minutes ago. "Excuse me."

Amber wasn't sure how long Jensen had been in the restaurant before she spotted him, but he hadn't kept his eyes off her for a moment.

About the time she was trying to snatch her hand out of Byerly's and tell him she was no cancan dancer and that she didn't care if the company was prepared to hire a dance instructor to help her prepare for the stupid audition, a cool British voice said, "Miss Rogers. What a surprise."

A flood of warmth rushed through her. She wished she could say it was the effects of Jose Cuervo making its way through her system, but she was afraid it was none other than Jensen Fortune Chesterfield who'd done the trick.

Either way, she welcomed the distraction and used it as her excuse to break away.

"I'm so glad you're here," she said, tearing her hand from the casting director's grip. "Mr. Byerly was just proposing a project he wanted me to consider, but I really need to get back to my table."

Just a few minutes ago, she'd called the ranch foreman and had asked someone to come and give Danny Boy a ride home. She hadn't planned on having a drink tonight—but then again, she hadn't expected to feel the need for one.

"You have my card," Byerly said. "Please call me."

"I told you I'd think about it. And I can't do that if you won't give me the time I need. So do us both a favor and let me be the one to make contact, okay?"

Once she'd left Byerly's table, she thanked Jensen for the interruption. "That guy doesn't take 'we'll see' for an answer."

"Then I'm glad I could help."

"I'm...uh, here with Gram—and Elmer Murdock, apparently. It seems my grandmother is full of surprises."

"Actually, I'm here with Orlando Mendoza and my mother. We just came in from the airfield, where we dropped off my sister and brother, who are heading back to London. When I saw you, I thought I'd come over and say hello."

Amber glanced at Gram, who'd lifted her hand and was waving her fingers at Jensen.

He'd no more than walked over to their table and greeted them when Elmer pointed toward the stairs, a gleam in his eyes. "Oh, Helen, look. Here come the Baumgartners. Let's go schmooze it up with them and find out what song they're planning for the dance contest. Keep your friends close and your enemies closer, I always say."

With that, Elmer pulled back Gram's chair and helped her to feet that had never danced even a two-step, at least as far as Amber knew.

But before he could sweep Helen away, Amber placed her hand on her grandmother's arm and asked, "Since when are you and Estelle Baumgartner enemies?"

"Elmer is just teasing, honey. He says they're our stiffest competition. Besides, I think he's just trying to give you and your young man some time alone."

"Try the twofer happy hour special, son. They make a mean margarita here, and you can't beat the price." Elmer winked at Jensen as he ushered Helen away, his gnarled hand a little too low on Gram's back.

Jensen was most certainly not her young man. And while she appreciated Elmer giving them some privacy, she didn't like him putting fanciful notions in her grandmother's head. It was bad enough the tabloids were spreading that rumor all over the county—and the world, for that matter.

"I hear they're having quite the bang-up price on them until seven o'clock." Jensen, still standing, nodded toward her margarita glass. "Can I get you another one of those frozen drinks?"

"Oh, goodness no. Thank you. I didn't even want this one."

He raised his eyebrow at her almost empty cup, as if questioning why she would've drunk the thing down in three gulps if she hadn't wanted it in the first place. And with the way he was looking down at her, she was reminded of the first time they met. Although this time, it was her neck hurting, not her pride.

"Are you sure you wouldn't like to sit down?" she asked.

"Maybe for a moment." He took the seat next to hers. "So how did the airport run go?"

"Without a snag. My brother and sister are on their way back across the pond as we speak."

"So you're staying on here a little longer?" She wanted him to think she was just making casual small talk and that his decision to stay in town wouldn't make the slightest bit of difference to her. It wouldn't, of course. But thoughts of that second kiss he'd given her after dropping her off near the VFW the other night made her insides turn to gelatin and her mouth go dry.

How did one explain the chemistry in a reaction like that?

Her hand shook as she reached for her empty glass. Well, duh. Now what? The only thing in front of her was the shot of tequila Elmer had ordered—the drink she hadn't planned on drinking.

Trying to play it cool, she downed that, then winced.

"Here." Jensen handed her his cold longneck bottle of beer.

She took a swig, then winced even more. "What is this?" She turned the label around and saw the harp logo on the front.

"It's Guinness. My cousin Wendy stocks up on it for us, since we're not used to the American ales. They're too watered-down."

Too watered-down? Was he crazy? Give her a cold light American beer any day over this thick drudge. But she bit her tongue as she handed his bottle back to him.

He signaled a waitress and asked her to bring another margarita and some water.

"Have my mother and Mr. Mendoza ordered yet?"

"No, sir. My lord. Um, I mean…" The young waitress stammered, most likely at a complete loss.

"Please, just call me Jensen. Will you let them know that I'll join them in a few moments?"

"Of course, Sir Jensen." The blushing woman hurried back to the bar.

As Amber watched her go, she wondered when the town would finally get used to this British invasion. The Beatles probably had it easier than the poor Fortune Chesterfields did.

"Speaking of your mom," Amber said, "Lady Josephine and Orlando seem to be hitting it off well."

"That's bloody unlikely." Jensen chuckled at the possibility. "Mum is just being social. She's quite the mingler. Besides, Mr. Mendoza and she are true opposites." He took a sip of his Guinness. "If she were to ever…well, become romantically involved with anyone, it would be with someone like my father. He was her soul mate—and one in a million." He paused and looked off in the distance.

In fact, he looked beyond Mr. Mendoza and Lady Josephine, who appeared so deep in conversation that they probably didn't even notice that Jensen was no longer sitting with them—much like Gram and Elmer did whenever Amber was around. Talk about a couple of third wheels. Amber had to laugh. Now that's something she and Jensen did have in common—the fact that they found themselves as odd men out.

"Anyway," the handsome blue blood continued, "why would my mum ever remarry when the only man she'd ever find would be someone who would fall short in her eyes?"

Amber looked over at the silver-haired British woman and the suave Orlando Mendoza. The two didn't seem to be all that mismatched to her.

But what did she know about romance or soul mates?

Then again, maybe Jensen was actually talking about his feelings for Amber—warning her that even though they shared a passionate kiss, he would never marry someone who clearly fell short in his eyes.

That had to be it. Okay, that was a no-brainer.

The waitress returned with the margarita that Amber didn't want, but she took a sip of it anyway to still her emotions and to cool whatever flush might have risen to the surface. But this time, she could blame it on the alcohol.

Fortunately, Gram and Elmer returned to save Amber from any further speculation of how unsuitable she and Jensen were.

As Elmer helped Gram into her seat, he said, "I'd have to say that me and Helen have the dance contest in the bag. They're going with Tony Bennett. Again. Talk about Snoozeville. I'll slip Clem Hodgkins a fiver to make sure we go after them. The Baumgartners will put the crowd to sleep, and then me and Helen will come along and bam! We'll wake 'em right back up."

Gram's laughter tinkled out, and Amber had to wonder if she was merely being polite, or if she actually enjoyed the old man's antics.

"So what music did you two select?" Jensen asked.

"Cotton-Eye Joe," Elmer said smugly.

Amber slapped her hand to her forehead.

"What?" Elmer asked. "Do you think it's too slow paced? Should we choose something livelier?"

Gram looked at her dancing partner, a furrow in her sweet brow, and Amber dumped the tequila shot into her margarita and took another drink. Heaven help her.

"Would you excuse me?" Jensen asked. "I need to tell

my mother and Orlando that I've temporarily jumped ship."

When he walked away, Elmer leaned forward and lowered his voice. "Did you do any fancy trick shooting for your audition?" Then he looked at Gram. "Maybe we should incorporate some pistols or something in our dance routine to really give it some pizzazz."

"No!" Amber nearly shot out of her seat. When the other diners turned to look at their table, she lowered her voice. "No, you two may not do any trick shooting. It's bad enough I have to worry about Gram breaking a hip, I don't want to worry about her accidentally shooting somebody's eye out."

"What's this about trick shooting?" Jensen asked, as he returned to the table.

"Amber is the best," Elmer said.

"Like Annie Oakley?" Jensen's smile was eager and almost hopeful.

The guy really needed to get a grip on this whole over-the-top Wild West fascination. Of course, it was people like him who would be paying customers, eager to see her show.

"Yes," Amber admitted, "but when I do trick shooting, it's in a controlled environment."

"Oh." The corners of his lips dropped and a look of dejection crossed his face. "So you don't really know how to shoot then."

Heck, the man acted as if she'd just told him Santa Claus wasn't real. "Of course I know how to shoot."

"A real gun?" His eyes sparkled with that same gleam Elmer's had right before he'd confronted the Baumgartners.

"Yes, a real gun. I'm an excellent shot."

"Care to make a wager on it?" Jensen smiled and cast a glance at Elmer, who'd scooted to the edge of his seat.

"I believe you still owe me from the last wager we made," she pointed out. Their barbecue date had understandably been waylaid by Amelia's recent delivery. And Amber had been looking forward to it.

"So then double or nothing," Elmer shouted out, having no idea what the bet was in the first place. The man just loved a competition.

Amber lifted her brow at Jensen, waiting to see how he would react to the old marine's suggestion.

But he didn't give it a second thought. "Yes. Double or nothing."

Chapter Six

Jensen wasn't sure what the old man had planned for today's shooting competition, but he knew one thing for certain—he had no plans of winning.

If he lost, he'd get to take Amber out on *two* dates, since he'd yet to collect on their original wager. And he'd been looking forward to their barbecue dinner.

Losing didn't come easy to a man who'd grown up competitive. And he'd never thrown a bet in his life.

But for Amber, the temptation had been far too great to resist.

He shook his head at the silly trail of thoughts. The bloody competition had yet to even begin and he'd already planned his surrender. The little Texas cowgirl was making his mind spin in funny directions. Something about her had him doing things he'd never think of doing back in England.

He rolled the window down. Maybe it wasn't Amber. Maybe it was something in the western breeze that blew tumbleweeds across the fields in summer and English bachelors willy-nilly in January.

Even his penchant for old cowboy movies couldn't explain the relaxing effects of being in Texas. And for once, overseeing the family investments and holdings, as well as Chesterfield Ltd., and keeping his siblings out of the tabloid limelight no longer seemed like the only things that mattered.

For some damned reason, he now found himself watching airplanes take off, riding horses on bulky Western saddles out to watering holes and kissing a rodeo queen behind a darkened feed store. He also found himself smiling for no reason at all, which he hadn't done since…well, in longer than he cared to ponder.

Now, as he eased Quinn's pickup along the dirt driveway and headed toward a parking area near the Broken R barn, he spotted Elmer Murdock and did a double take.

The stocky, elderly was man toting liter-sized bottles of soda out of the back of the spiffed-up muscle car. But why was he dressed like a leprechaun playing in a polo match at the VFW hall?

Jensen parked and exited the truck.

The old man, wearing tight white jodhpurs on his short, bowed legs, waved him over. "Top o' the morning to ya."

As Jensen made his way to Mr. Murdock's open trunk, the elderly man handed him a crate holding eight plastic bottles filled with bright neon-pink soda.

Jensen looked at the array of containers. What in the

world was he doing with so much…? He glanced at the label. Caliente Pepper Fiz?

"Were they having a special at the grocery?" Jensen asked.

"They sure was, but not at the Superette here in town. I picked these up over at the discount drug place on the way to Lubbock. Seems they didn't sell as well as store-owners hoped, so they were just sitting on a pallet out back, expiring in the sun."

"Did they go bad in the heat?" That would explain the unnatural neon-pink color.

"I don't reckon so. This here is their strawberry-cream-flavored line. The regular hot sauce flavored soda is pretty tasty, but no one seemed to like it much when they added the strawberries to the original mix."

Jensen looked again at the label. These Texans and their food products could sure be inventive. "Hmm. You'd think they wouldn't be able to keep hot sauce-flavored cola on the shelf."

"I know," Mr. Murdock said, not recognizing Jensen's sarcasm. "Oh well, it's the Caliente Company's loss and our gain, right ol' chap?"

Jensen was raised to be polite, but there was no bet in the world that would make him drink strawberry-cream-and-hot-sauce-flavored cola—let alone nearly fifty bottles of the wretched stuff. "Tell me why it's our gain?"

"They make perfect targets, son. When your bullet hits one of these suckers, boom! Hot-pink juice explodes everywhere. Not only is it fun to look at, it saves the range master some footwork. He doesn't have to run back and forth to measure the targets. And since that'll be my job for this here competition, I figured I'll save my legs for that upcoming dance contest."

Just then, Amber stepped out of the ranch house cradling a rifle and a box of ammunition.

She looked just as serious as Wyatt Earp himself making his way to the OK Corral. Of course, Wyatt Earp didn't look as sexy. Her snug jeans hugged her curvy hips, tempting a man to want to go out and buy her a dress… Or maybe some silky lingerie.

Jensen came to a complete stop, not even noticing the weight of the bottles in his arms as he watched Amber walk toward him. She wore a shiny silver belt buckle along a tiny waist a man could span his hands—

"Are you ready to get beat by a girl, Sir Jensen?" she asked.

He forced himself to pull his gaze away from her dangerous torso to her seductive brown eyes. And to be honest, if he was ever ready get bested by a girl, it was today. And it was this girl. Or rather, this woman. No doubt about that.

His throat worked to swallow, but his mouth was so dry he almost opened one of the discolored sodas and took a huge sip.

What a mistake that would be.

Back in London, he'd never been tongue-tied around the beautiful socialites and jet-setters who made up his social circle. Then again, they didn't have anyone quite like Amber Rogers in the British Isles—or all of Europe, for that matter.

A hand smacked against his back, pitching him forward. "Keep it moving, son. I got an appointment with my podiatrist at one o'clock to see about my bunions. And if I win our bet, Helen said she'd go with me afterward to that remodeled movie theater over in Vicker's Corners."

Jensen picked up his pace, hoping Mr. Murdock wouldn't miss out on his opportunity to squire Helen to the cinema.

Because there was no way Jensen was going to miss out on his own date with Amber. Instead he said, "I appreciate your vote of confidence."

"Hell, son," Murdock said. "I didn't bet on *you*. I bet on our Amber over there."

Amber's hand held steady as she chambered the first, which was surprising since she'd caught the ways Jensen had studied the jeans she normally saved for when she wasn't working on the ranch. At first, she'd thought he might be assessing her choice of clothing, since the uptight Brit was so stoic and difficult for her to read.

But riding the pro rodeo circuit provided her with plenty of opportunity to study the male species and their mating rituals. And there appeared to be one thing that applied to all men around the world. They couldn't hide their sexual interest in their eyes.

Whether Jensen was wearing a top hat or a Stetson or no head covering at all—like today, with just the Texas breeze to ruffle his dark locks—the intensity in his gaze couldn't mask his obvious physical attraction.

Nor did Amber want it to. It caught her off guard and made her tremble as she walked toward the makeshift range Elmer had set up alongside the barn. It even filled her head with intoxicating ideas of what that gaze could lead to. It also made her feel like a desirable worldly woman, one who hadn't given up her career to breed horses at the family ranch in the middle of Texas.

She didn't know what it all meant, but she certainly liked the way it made her feel, the way it made her walk a little taller and with a little more sway to her hips. And she'd be darned if she wouldn't win this shooting competition and have a night on the town with him because in no time at all, he'd return to London, leaving her in Horseback Hollow, where she'd be forced to read about his dates—rumored or real—in all the tabloids.

She'd once dreamed of riding the rodeo, traveling the world and tasting all it had to offer. And she did accomplish her goal—sort of, given that she'd never made it outside the borders of North America. Jensen provided a glimpse into that lifestyle that she would never have. But Horseback Hollow and the Broken R had always been home to her. And when push came to shove, she'd always known she'd end up back here one day anyway.

And if that meant she had to shoot her best today to get a small taste of glamour for two nights at best, then that's exactly what she would do.

So she lifted the stock to her shoulder, took careful aim at the Caliente soda bottle and squeezed the trigger.

"Hot damn!" Elmer shrieked as the neon pink liquid sprayed into the air.

Gram clapped politely from her seat off to the side. "Three more shots to go."

Amber made all of them, blasting strawberry-cream-and-hot-sauce-flavored soda with each direct hit.

"That's our girl!" The retired marine patted her back, then hurried out to place new targets for Jensen's turn.

Amber passed the rifle over to her competitor and smiled.

"Well-done, Miss Rogers." Jensen loaded the shotgun, took aim and shot through the bottle, blasting a spray of pink liquid. Then he turned to her and winked. "I prefer the British Boss over the American Remington, but I believe this rifle will get the job done."

Amber crossed her arms. "We'll see who's 'boss' when it comes to shooting then, won't we?"

"So we shall. And to be perfectly honest, I'd enjoy competing with you just to have what you Americans call bragging rights."

"We'll see who's bragging when it's all said and done, Sir Jensen."

He flashed her a handsome grin, then proceeded to fire again, nailing the next two targets.

Amber's pulse rate soared. She'd always enjoyed the adrenaline rush of competition—friendly or otherwise. But this was different. Each time Jensen cast a glance her way, his brow lifted, his lips quirked in a boyish grin, a glimmer in his eyes, her heart did all kinds of loop-de-loops.

Talk about a rush...

As Jensen took aim at the last target and drew back on the trigger, he pulled his right shoulder back a bit too much, and his round veered into the fence post.

"Whoop-dee-doo!" Elmer shouted. "We won!" He lifted Amber into the air and twirled her around in his stocky arms.

While she appreciated Elmer's support and enthusiasm, she didn't want to rub Jensen's loss in his face. She might be a born competitor, but she was also a good sport.

So was Jensen, it seemed, because losing didn't seem to bother him at all. In fact, a smile tugged at his lips, and a glimmer lit his eyes. Surely he hadn't missed his last shot on purpose...?

When Jensen set down the rifle, and Elmer set her down to hurry over to Gram, Amber held out her right hand.

"Good game," she said.

Jensen accepted her offer of sportsmanship with grace and class, although he held her hand a bit longer than necessary, and his smile deepened. "Make sure you wear those jeans when we go to dinner."

With that, he released her, but his gaze held her steady and tight—so much so that she had to will herself to take a breath. Finally she glanced down at her Wrangler jeans. "Why do you want me to wear these?"

"They're a nice fit."

She'd been thinking about wearing a dress, but maybe he hadn't meant their dinner date to be a...date.

"All right. It's a da...deal."

Jensen glanced toward the back porch, where Gram was sitting, smiling with Elmer, and winked.

Amber was more surprised to see that it was Gram who actually returned Jensen's wink.

Amber walked into Smokey Joe's, her favorite barbecue joint and honky-tonk in Lubbock. Normally the place was bright and loud during the dinner rush, then the staff moved the tables and dimmed the lights. That's when the drinkers and line dancers showed up.

She wore new boots—and the jeans Jensen hadn't been able to keep his eyes off that morning. She also found a black, ruffled halter top in the back of her closet and threw a short suede jacket over it. She doubted Jensen would be up for any dancing afterward, but she dressed in layers, just in case.

It may be cool outside, but when the crowds settled

in and the music got going, small places like Smokey
Joe's could heat up quickly.

She was met by the hostess, a peppy college-age girl
with a vivacious smile, a low-cut blouse and a pair of
Daisy Duke–style shorts.

"I'm meeting someone," Amber said.

The young woman, whose name tag read *Maddie*
and whose legs looked as if they could use a lot more
covering than what the skimpy denim provided, smiled.
"A tall, formal, good-looking dude?"

At Smokey Joe's? That description couldn't possibly describe anyone else. Amber nodded, then followed
the hostess.

For the eighth time that night, she wondered if she'd
put on too much makeup or if she'd overdressed. She ran
a hand through her long and loose hair, wishing she'd
clipped it back or pinned it up.

This wasn't a date. And she didn't want Jensen getting the idea that she was trying to dress to impress him.
But it was too late to change course now, so she continued on, past the makeshift seating on the dance floor
and then the bar itself. They even passed the kitchen
with its open window letting out scents of smoked meat
and tangy sauce.

She'd eaten here plenty of times, but she had no idea
there was more seating this far back. Where the heck
was Maddie the hostess taking her?

Maybe she'd misunderstood. Maybe there were two
tall, handsome, formal dudes in this neck of the woods.

Dang, maybe there was some private party going
on, and Amber was about to crash it. But just as they
rounded a corner, Jensen, who'd been seated at a small

table in a hidden alcove, stood to greet her. "Hello, Amber."

She looked around, still curious about this secluded corner. "Well, what do you know? I had no idea they had a room back here."

"I thought it would be quieter than out front."

And a lot more private. Did he do this sort of thing with all his dates?

Not a date! she reminded herself—and with a mental scolding.

He pulled out a chair for her and she took a seat. "I took the liberty of ordering a margarita with the tequila shot in it for you. You seemed to enjoy them when Mr. Murdock ordered them for you at the cantina."

Great. Just what she needed—the possibility of losing all her inhibitions with the man. She should advise him not to take dating cues from Elmer Murdock.

Instead, she smiled and thanked him for his thoughtfulness.

Maddie handed them the menus. "Your waiter will be with you shortly. I'll let him know where you are."

You'd better. Something told her they could be left to die back here until closing time.

She scanned the area, where they were the only diners. "I wonder why they put us way out to pasture."

"Oh, that was at my request. I asked them for something more private, where there would be less risk of being bothered by others."

"You know, part of the barbecue experience is the communal tables and environment. I mean, I know this place isn't swanky, but it has good food."

"I can ask the hostess to reseat us, if you'd rather be in the dining hall area. I just assumed you would want to be away from the prying eyes of the public, and I didn't want any more cameras catching us doing something as innocuous as sharing a meal."

She hated to sound ungrateful. Besides, she didn't want him to be uncomfortable if he preferred their out-of-the-way table. "No, this is fine."

Although, it was much warmer back here. They must be sitting on the other side of the kitchen with its hot smoking pits. She took off her jacket and hung it on the back of her chair before turning and catching the surprised look on his face.

He was staring at her blouse, and suddenly, she was glad she'd done so much riding and roping recently because she knew her shoulders and tight arms were her best features.

A waiter in a black Stetson came to take their order. "Wow. I heard we had a celebrity back here, but they didn't say who it was."

"I trust you'll keep it to yourself until after we leave," Jensen said.

"I sure will." The young man cast a smile at Amber. "But I don't suppose I could get your autograph before you go, Miss Rogers. It isn't every day that we get a rodeo queen in here."

She smiled. "Of course, you can."

The waiter's cheeks flushed. "My sister was a huge fan and followed your career. She even tried to barrel-race like you. 'Course she isn't nearly as pretty as you are."

"Thank you." Amber glanced at Jensen, whose expression had grown serious.

After the waiter took their orders and returned to the kitchen, Jensen said, "Maybe we should move. It was cooler on the other side of the restaurant, and then you'd be able to keep your jacket on."

"No, truly, this table is fine." Didn't Jensen like her top? He definitely didn't seem to like their waiter, who'd continued to study her while they'd ordered.

After the waiter finally served their drinks, Jensen took a long draw from his bottle of Heineken, since there weren't any stout British ales served here.

He chugged another long gulp.

Was something still bothering him?

Maybe she was reading too much into his expression.

"How's Amelia feeling?" she asked, wanting to get back on neutral territory.

He looked up, his serious demeanor fading into a slow smile. "Quite well. She's glad to finally have baby Clementine home."

"I can imagine. I once had to go to the hospital to get my appendix out, and I couldn't wait to leave. I missed everything about home, from Gram's cooking to my horse. I promised to stay in bed for a week if the doctor would just let me leave, which was a pretty big promise for a twelve-year-old girl with a new horse and an up-coming junior state barrel-racing competition to make."

"And when they finally did release you, did you stay in bed?"

"For one whole day. Pop caught me sneaking out to the stables a couple days later and let me ride for a few minutes before Gram found out and lit into us something fierce."

"Your sweet grandmother? I can't imagine her yelling."

"She didn't need to. She told one of the ranch hands to take Miss Muffin, my new horse, over to the Drummonds' place so I couldn't ride her. Then she went on strike in the kitchen, making Pop eat frozen dinners and cereal for the next two weeks to remind him that being an accomplice to a twelve-year-old's whims, especially when she was recovering from surgery, wasn't his smartest move. Needless to say, both Pop and I learned our lesson."

"So you didn't get to go to the junior state rodeo?"

"No, I still got to go, but I'd barely had any practice beforehand, so neither Miss Muffin nor I were up to speed. Literally. I came in second place to Starlight from Vicker's Corners."

"Well, then it all worked out well in the end."

"No, it was the worst moment of my life. I hate coming in second place. And I hated it even more that snotty Molly Watkins won the buckle that should have been mine if it hadn't been for my stupid appendix getting in the way of my training schedule. She was so smug with her perfectly curled red hair and expensive outfit that was better suited to a homecoming queen than a barrel racer."

A glimmer lit Jensen's eyes. "A bad sport, then, this Molly girl?"

"The worst. She told everyone that the reason I didn't do well was because I'd tried to kiss Billy Carmichael behind the warm-up fences, and he'd pushed me away, making me too upset to do my ride."

Jensen, who'd clearly been engaged in their conversation before, leaned forward. "Who was Billy Carmichael?"

Surely he wasn't the least bit jealous of a thirteen-year-old boy—but she liked the idea that he might be interested in her romantic history—as short and unremarkable as it had been. "Billy's dad was one of the rodeo clowns, and Billy was the top calf roper at the National Little Britches Rodeo Finals two years running. Let's just say that for a junior high school girl, he was a big deal."

"So Billy Carmichael didn't defend your honor?"

"Nope. He liked everyone thinking that I had a crush on him."

"What a cad."

"Exactly."

Jensen smiled, and her heart picked up speed. She took a drink of her margarita. With the way he was looking at her, she would've downed the whole thing. Luckily, the waiter, whose name tag read *Danny*, brought their food just then—as well as a sheet of paper he'd printed out with a photo of her in her barrel racing days.

She signed it to Bonnie Sue, wishing her all the best in her career.

"Would you mind posing for a photo?" Danny asked.

"Yes, we'd mind," Jensen said.

Danny's shoulders slumped. "I'm sorry. I didn't mean to interrupt your dinner. I could come back afterward."

"I asked for this table because I like my privacy," Jensen said. "I don't want my picture taken."

"Sorry, sir." Danny said again. "I didn't want you in it. I was hoping you'd take a shot of Amber and me with the camera in my cell phone."

Amber laughed. It served Jensen right to realize there were some people more popular in Texas than a British noble. "Be a sport. It'll only take a minute to make a girl's day."

And it did.

Moments later, after the happy waiter went back to

the kitchen, Amber and Jensen dug into their meals. "So, did you ever get back at Molly what's-her-name?" Jensen asked after spearing a bite of cooked rib tips.

"I got back at her every year after that. In the arena, that is. I never came in second to Molly Watkins again."

Jensen laughed, and Amber tried the Campfire Beans.

"Oh, didn't you order any of these?" she asked, looking at his plate.

"No, I chose the homemade coleslaw and the Belt-Bustin' Baked Potato. And they're very good. You were right. This is the best barbecue restaurant I've been to yet, although I'm afraid I'm still what you'd call a novice."

"Here, try this." She spooned a taste of seasoned beans into his mouth.

He reciprocated by giving her one of his rib tips.

They talked and shared food with each other as if they'd had countless dinners together. She fed him macaroni salad. He buttered cornbread and held it up to her mouth.

It wasn't until the meal was over that Amber realized they could've easily just used their own utensils and eaten off each other's plates. They didn't have to feed one another.

She rubbed her bare arms, suddenly embarrassed at the shared intimacy.

Jensen's eyes focused again on her skimpy top just as a fiddle player started warming up in the main dining room.

"Looks like the band is getting ready." She felt a little silly for pointing out the obvious.

"Do you dance much?" he asked.

"I can hold my own. What about you?" She hoped he'd invite her to two-step.

"Yes, but not to this. Frankly, this may come as a surprise to you, but they don't teach us country-and-western line dancing in cotillion class."

"Really? And yet the waltz is so terribly popular in my neck of the woods." She smiled, just as the band launched into full swing.

"Shall we have a dance-off then, Miss Rogers?" he asked as he scraped his chair back and offered his hand.

"I'd love to." She pushed aside the Jose Cuervo she hadn't touched and rose to join him. "But I should warn you." She leaned toward him, her mouth aimed toward his ear as he guided her to the dance floor. "One day soon I aim to do a mean cancan."

She caught herself the moment the words rolled out of her mouth, especially since she was merely entertaining the idea, especially after drinking a margarita.

"The cancan? My goodness, Miss Rogers. You're full of surprises. I'd love to see that sometime—especially if you're in costume."

Gram planned to work on her fancy outfit, and if Amber gave her the go-ahead, that was something Jensen would never see. So she laughed off her slip of the tongue.

As she stood, Jensen said, "Don't forget your coat."

"Are you crazy? It's too hot to think about wearing something like that on the dance floor." She did, however, take her purse, which was a tiny little bag barely able to hold her keys, her ID, a credit card and some cash.

Jensen seemed to study her momentarily, and she patted the purse that hung at her side by a narrow shoulder strap. "I travel light when I plan to spend some time on a dance floor."

He seemed to ponder that a moment, then spun her into his arms. A beat later, they joined the others two-stepping across the parquet floor.

Jensen did much better than she'd expected, and they were soon laughing and twirling their way around to various renditions of classic George Strait and Alan Jackson songs.

After the first set, the band paused for a break. She'd worked up a thirst. Jensen asked if she wanted to order another margarita, but since she was driving, she told him she'd prefer a glass of ice water to cool her down.

"This has been the most enjoyable night I've had since my arrival in Texas," Jensen said, then he leaned in closer. "You're an excellent dancer, Amber. And an enjoyable companion."

She told herself that the loud music had forced them to talk into each other's ears the past hour, and that they leaned into each other as a matter of habit.

"Companion, huh?" she said, maintaining the intimate proximity.

He glanced at the top she wore, which helped to keep her cool in the heated quarters. But there was another kind of closeness, another heat that had her steamed up. Him, too, it seemed.

When a cowboy walked by, carrying a longneck bottle of beer, he gave her a flirtatious grin and tipped his hat. But he hadn't really meant anything by it. She was used to being recognized.

Jensen's smile faded. "There are too many people ogling us in here. Maybe we should go outside. Why don't you get your jacket?"

Just who was he to be concerned about them ogling? He certainly hadn't staked his claim, and even if he had, she wasn't about to let anyone tell her what she could and couldn't wear out in public. The blouse wasn't all that skimpy!

And while she wouldn't mind going outside anyway, she fought the urge to go for her jacket. Her rebellious streak wouldn't allow it, especially since Jensen was doing that judgmental upper-crust thing again, like he'd done that first day she'd met him on his sister's porch.

That being the case, he'd need to learn that she wasn't going to be intimated by him or his snobby attitude. "Apparently you don't like my top."

"It's fine."

The female singer stepped onto stage just as the chords for a Patsy Cline song sounded over the speakers. Couples made their way back onto the dance floor, but Jensen stood facing her—and looking down his aristocratic nose.

"If you were Pinocchio, your nose would stretch out a foot right now. And birds would be swooping down to build a nest on it."

"There's not a bloody thing wrong with your blouse," he said. "Which is why every man in this place has been staring at you."

She looked around. The cowboy was long gone by now, and she didn't see anyone else staring at her, other than a man in a John Deere hat near the bar. But that guy was probably watching the scene they were causing rather than the way her shirt rose above her waistline.

She uncrossed her arms, tucked her thumbs in her front pockets and shifted her weight to one hip. "Nobody is staring at me, Jensen. And so what if they were?"

"You know what? You're right. So what if they are? They can stare all they like because you're here with *me*. And the sooner all the other single guys find that out, the better."

He wrapped his arm around her waist and pulled her onto the dance floor, holding her close as the singer belted out lines about being crazy for loving you.

She tried not to think of what he was so all-fired worked up about. Was it really *her*?

Truth be told, she fancied being locked in his embrace all night long. And if, down the road, things blew up in their faces, it would serve the both of them right for playing with fire. They were a mismatched pair— and nothing could ever come of it.

So why did she even harbor the slightest little dream that things could be different? But clearly, they weren't.

Before she could wonder about Jensen's intentions, the man in the John Deere hat held up his smartphone, the flash of the camera going off.

Chapter Seven

Jensen took Amber's hand and led her off the dance floor, through the throng of people who'd gathered around to watch the cowboys and their dates slow dancing to the sounds of "Crazy," and out of Smokey Joe's.

As they moved, Amber scanned their surroundings. "The guy who took the photo isn't following us. And he wasn't one of the reporters who was at Quinn's ranch the other day."

"If he was one of the paparazzi, he'd be out here now, snapping more photos."

"Then why did we have to leave?"

"Because I wasn't up for a photo shoot—no matter who was behind the lens—or what kind of camera it was."

Besides, amateurs sold photographs to the tabloids all the time—something the Fortune Chesterfields knew too well.

Jensen slowed their pace as they were outside and in the clear, then he walked Amber to her pickup.

"If you don't mind," she said, "I'd like my jacket now."

"I'll go back inside for it."

She crossed her arms, ignoring the gooseflesh which had risen to the surface of her skin. "Not so fast. What's the deal, Jensen?"

"You're going to freeze out here. Are you just plain contrary?"

"It's the principle. I make my own choices when it comes to my wardrobe—and to my inner thermostat. When I was hotter than blazes inside, you wanted me covered up. And I'd like to know why."

"Sorry. I just didn't like seeing all the men in there ogling you."

She lifted a brow. "But it's okay for *you* to do it?"

When she stated it that way, he supposed it wasn't. Although he liked the black lacy blouse—and the way it revealed her tiny waist and sexy midriff.

But he wasn't being the least bit fair, was he? Not when there wasn't a chance in hell that the two of them would make any kind of match—lasting or otherwise.

Well, perhaps otherwise might be an option, but he'd be damned if he knew how to broach a subject like that. He might have his share of ladies offering to be his lovers, but he wasn't what you'd call a Casanova.

He'd never had to be.

Yet, again, that wasn't fair to Amber. So if their friendship or relationship went in that direction, the decision would have to be hers to make.

"I had a lovely evening," he said.

She stopped, turned, slapped her hands on her

denim-clad hips and completely disarmed him with a look of astonishment. "Did you just completely ignore my question?"

"The one about your top and how sexy I found it this evening? Why, yes. I was moving on to a safer topic."

"And my sexy blouse is dangerous because…?"

She was provoking him, setting him up. Prompting him to continue.

All right. He'd take the bait. Perhaps it would lead to the direction he'd like things to take—her choice, of course.

"Because a conversation like that would surely lead to me kissing you senseless in the parking lot, especially since we seem to be the only two out here, without any witnesses to sully your reputation."

For a couple of heartbeats, silence played cat and mouse in the moonlight.

"And kissing me would be a bad thing?" she asked.

"You tell me."

With that, the lovely, irrepressible and delightful Miss Amber Rogers—no relation to either Roy or Rod—did better than that.

She showed him by rising up on tiptoe, wrapping her arms around his neck and kissing him…utterly senseless.

Her scent—something that reminded him of ripe peaches in full harvest—enveloped him. His hands sought to draw her close, to hold her, to capture the essence of the woman who tempted him beyond reason, while his tongue dipped and twisted and mated with hers.

Then, just as quickly as it all started, she pulled her sweet lips from his, dropped her arms and spun around.

Before he could blink or think, she reached into her tiny purse, pulled out a key fob and said, "I'll see you later." Then she climbed into her pickup and turned the ignition as if nothing between them had happened.

And perhaps it hadn't. Because a couple of heartbeats later, she drove off, leaving him standing in the moonlight, bewitched, bothered and more than a little befuddled.

It had taken every ounce of Amber's strength and willpower to control her weak knees, trembling arms and pounding heart to leave as if she was completely unaffected by that good-night kiss. But what she might lack in sexual experience and worldliness, she made up for in gumption.

Jensen may have thought he'd made her feel better about things, but he hadn't. And that's mostly because there was a whole lot he didn't know, a whole lot she hadn't told him.

How would he react when everyone in town, including the *Cross Town Crier*, learned that she'd accepted the job of riding in the Cowboy Country USA Wild West Show? Or that she'd been asked to audition for a part in Madame LaRue's Lone Star Review—which meant donning a saloon-girl costume that Gram was stitching up for her because Elmer Murdock suggested it would give her a "leg up"—the pun very much intended?

Not that she'd decided to try out for sure. But doggone it. She was certainly tempted to do just that because she could almost hear Patrick Swayze's voice booming out in the cab of her truck: *No one puts Amber in a corner.*

Okay, so *Dirty Dancing* had always been one of her mom's favorite movies, and Amber had watched the DVD a hundred times.

But bottom line? Amber was both a competitor and maybe even an entertainer at heart. And she wasn't meant to spend her entire life marooned on a ranch. Of course, that didn't mean she didn't love the Broken R or Horseback Hollow or Texas, for that matter. They would always be home to her.

It's just that, deep down in her heart, she'd wanted to shine and to be someone. And now Cowboy Country USA was providing her an opportunity to have it all. Well, if Jensen ever got wind of her involvement, that would surely put the end to anything that might come of any romantic opportunities there.

But who was she kidding?

A few heated kisses didn't mean anything without an invitation to go along with them. And at this rate, this *thing* or *friendship* or whatever you wanted to call it, wasn't apt to go anywhere—nor was it going to last more than a week or two at the most.

And even if they did sneak off and do more than just kiss, the whole thing would fizzle out soon enough. They were a mismatched pair—and nothing could ever come of it.

So why did she dare even harbor the slightest little hope that things could be different?

Actually, the way he wanted to keep things secret made her mad as heck and fired her up.

Who whisked their dates out under the cover of darkness to a quaint little out-of-the-way place, treated them to a romantic dinner and shared a soul-stirring, knee-wobbling good-bye kiss only to let them go their own way?

Okay, so she'd been the one to leave. And just like Cinderella at the ball, she'd left her suede jacket behind when she ran off in a rush to escape the inevitable reality of the situation.

He'd called her an hour later to make sure she'd gotten home all right and to tell her he had her suede jacket. She'd thanked him, and they'd made small talk for a while, although they didn't broach anything remotely serious, like jealousy or heated kisses.

But she clearly wasn't Jensen's type. Nor did she belong in his world. She was a fool to even entertain a fleeting dream that they could ever share more than a few sneaky dates and a couple of stolen kisses.

And Gram and Pop didn't raise her to be no fool.

Amber pulled the rig into the side yard just after dark. It had been a long day and she'd just delivered a couple of cutting horses to one of their clients on a ranch near Lubbock.

Normally, she wouldn't be so exhausted so early in the evening, but she hadn't been able to sleep last night after dancing with Jensen and remembering how good it felt to be held in his arms.

Or how his kiss had rocked her to the core.

As she shut off the ignition, she noticed the green Dodge Charger parked near the back door. The light was still on in the kitchen.

Obviously, Gram had company for dinner. Again.

It's not that Amber minded Elmer being at their house so much lately. It was just that she didn't want to have to make conversation tonight or have the perceptive old man quiz her about Jensen and about what he suspected might be going on between them.

Because the truth of the matter was, even if Amber wanted to be perfectly open and up-front, she didn't have an answer for him—or for anyone.

While she'd worked the horses this morning and then during the drive both to and from the ranch near Lubbock, she'd run the whole situation backward and forward in her mind. Yet, she still had trouble knowing what to make of it all—the fun she had when they were together, the attraction she felt for him, the sexual feeling he aroused in her. And he seemed to be experiencing those same things—although she could certainly be reading into that all wrong.

Sometimes, when she found herself losing focus or direction, she'd put on headphones and pump Garth Brooks as loud as she could stand it, just to help her mind clear. And if her mind ever needed some clearing, it was tonight.

Yet, cruising down the highway, with the horse trailer hitched behind, the last thing she wanted to be reminded about was how things between her and Jensen could never work out. So when Garth had come on the radio, singing about Papa lovin' Mama into an early grave, she'd switched the dial to a loud rock station. There'd be no songs about fatal attractions or star-crossed lovers for her tonight.

Now, as she walked toward the front porch, her ears were still ringing from the electric guitars that had blasted the entire ride home.

She didn't want to deal with Gram or Elmer Murdock or even the empty horse trailer she'd left hitched to the truck. All she wanted was a piece of Gram's leftover cornbread and maybe a cold glass of milk before taking a nice hot shower and hitting the sheets.

When she entered the house, she spotted Elmer resting comfortably in Pop's old leather recliner. So comfortably, in fact, that his age-spotted hands were crossed over his extended belly and his mouth hung wide open. His snores were loud enough to trigger the lowering of the guardrail on a railroad track.

Amber didn't appreciate another man taking Pop's place in the ranch house, but at least Elmer was sound asleep. Thank goodness for small favors.

She heard the sink water shut off, so she made her way into the kitchen, where Gram was drying dishes with an old flour sackcloth.

Helen Rogers always claimed a woman did her best thinking standing in front of a kitchen sink. And Amber had found that to be true, as well. In fact, the kitchen was a special place. Some of their best conversations happened right there on that worn spot of pine boards in front of the faucet. So she picked up another cloth and took a wet plate from the dish rack, as Gram turned and greeted her with a warm smile.

"I see you've got company." Amber nodded her head toward the living room, where the television hummed with the nightly newscast.

"Poor Elmer plum tuckered himself out today, so I figured I'd let him rest up before he had to drive home."

"How'd he wear himself out?" Amber asked, before she could stop herself. She didn't mean to imply that the man was lazy. A tornado couldn't keep up with him. But he was clearly basking in Snoozeville while Gram was cleaning up.

Of course, Pop never had lifted a finger around the

house, since it had always been Gram's domain, but still, he'd worked hard on the ranch.

"Elmer cooked dinner," Gram said. "He made an amazing beef Wellington and the most delicious fingerling potatoes. He even baked a chocolate soufflé for dessert. You wouldn't guess it by the way he won that chicken wing–eating contest over at the Moose Lodge last week, but he's quite the gourmet."

No, Amber wouldn't believe it. And she was tempted to check the fridge to see if there were any leftovers in there to prove it. But she'd take Gram's word for it.

"So how did the delivery go?" Gram asked, thankfully changing the subject.

"Pretty well. Stumpy Thomas was pleased with the gelding, and his granddaughter went nuts over the young mare. He cut me a check while I was there, so if you're going into town tomorrow, could you swing by the bank?"

"Well, I do have that tea planned with the garden committee. It's not even spring and already they're planning for the Blue Ribbon Floral Spectacular. Elmer thinks my roses are going to bloom early this year. And he was online all yesterday afternoon researching alternative fertilizing techniques."

Amber couldn't see the old man maneuvering his way around the World Wide Web, but he certainly knew his way around winning competitions he had no business entering. So if Elmer was backing Gram's rose bushes, that blue ribbon was as good as hers.

"So what's going on with you and Elmer, anyway?" Amber asked as she put away a bowl and reached for the wet silverware. *Please say you're just friends.*

"I guess the same thing that's going on with you

and that Sir Jensen you've been spending so much time with."

Sure, Amber told everyone she and Jensen were just friends, and while things had definitely been getting a lot more than friendly between them, she didn't want to think that something similar between Gram and the retired marine might be heating up, as well. Gross.

But since Amber didn't want to have *that* conversation with her grandmother, she kept her mouth closed.

After a couple of minutes, Gram dried her hands and took off her apron. Then she turned to Amber. "Why don't you like Elmer?"

"It's not that. I've always enjoyed his humor. Who doesn't? He's very entertaining. But as far as the two of you go, I guess I just don't get what *you* find so appealing about him."

"He has a romantic streak."

Amber glanced over her shoulder and into the living room at the snoring old coot. "You gotta be kidding."

"This afternoon, he took me to the Golden Horseshoe, the old theater that was refurbished last fall, the one offering old classics at a low price."

"You found that romantic? The place charges three bucks to see super old movies that you can watch on TV for free."

"But it's not the same as sitting side by side, sharing Milk Duds in the dark and watching them on the big screen."

Amber took another look at the man and wondered if sticky caramels were good for his dentures, which were, at this very moment, at risk of sliding out of his slack mouth.

"Plus," Gram added, "on Sundays they do a senior

special. And Elmer said he saved five dollars on our tickets and popcorn combo."

Not that Pop had been rolling in the dough, but Gram deserved a nicer date than some discount movie theater. Of course, Mr. Murdock was probably on a limited income with his military retirement, but did he have to be so obvious in his money-saving techniques?

"Okay," Amber said, deciding to focus on the positive. "I'll give you that the theater definitely has ambiance. So what did you see?"

"Urban Cowboy."

"And you thought *that* was romantic?"

"Actually, yes. Have you ever seen it?"

Amber nodded. "Once. About a year ago, when I couldn't sleep. It was on television. The music was pretty cool—for an old classic—but I can think of a lot better romantic movies."

"Do you remember how Bud, John Travolta's character, used to drive Sissy around town in his truck?"

"Debra Winger played Sissy, right? I remember that. He had that big black Ford with those little personalized souvenir license plates in the back window. What about it?"

"Come with me." Gram motioned for Amber to follow her out to the mudroom, where the porch light illuminated the back steps. Still, she reached into the cupboard and withdrew a flashlight before taking Amber outside.

When they reached the Dodge Charger, Gram walked around to the back and flashed the light on the rear window, where someone had painted *Elmer* on the driver's side and *Helen* on the passenger side with a cursive flair.

"He had it done while we were at the movie theater," Gram said. "Rod Rogers, from the paint and body shop, came over as a favor to him, and did it while we were inside. Isn't that the sweetest thing you ever did see?"

Oh, for Pete's sake.

Okay, maybe it was a little romantic, but did Amber really want her sweet and prim grandmother hot-rodding around town in that green death machine with her name emblazoned across the back?

"So what does this mean? Are you and—" Amber pointed to his painted name "—are an official item?"

"Oh, I don't know what to call it. We're too old to worry about labels and nonsense like that. All I know is that Elmer makes me feel special, and I like spending time with him."

"But now everyone in town will know that you guys are together. These new graphics make quite the statement, Gram."

The older woman reached over and patted her hand. "Dear, I know it's not as subtle as, oh, say, a front-page picture spread on an international tabloid."

"Point taken," Amber said, shoulders slumping. "But he's just so different from Pop."

"What's wrong with different?"

Everything, right?

Before Amber could begin to list the reasons people searched for soul mates, her cell phone rang. She was half tempted to ignore it, but decided to check the display first.

Jensen?

"Just a minute, Gram. I need to take this." She swept her finger across the screen, accepting the call. "Hey. What's up?"

"Not much. I just wondered if you'd like to go out on a date."

She smiled, and her heart lightened. "A *real* one?"

"Yes, and then we can go to dinner afterward. But it might be wiser if you met me."

"Of course. I understand. Where?"

"At the Golden Horseshoe Theater."

Was this a joke?

"Seriously?" she asked.

"I heard it was unique and a lot of fun."

And Amber had given Gram a hard time about Elmer Murdock taking her to that ol' place with the two-bit movies.

"What's the matter?" Jensen asked.

"Nothing. I was just wondering why you'd suggest we meet there."

"Elmer told me it's quite the rage. And while I was in town earlier today, I noticed a flyer advertising a movie I'd like to see."

Amber didn't know what to say. The Golden Horseshoe had to be "quite the rage" at the VFW or the Moose Lodge or the senior center because none of her friends had mentioned it.

"Are you busy tomorrow night?" Jensen asked.

"No."

"Then would you like to join me?"

It wasn't that. She was trying to figure out if he was stringing her along. Or just what the heck was behind all of this sneaky, I'll-meet-you business.

Was his real reason for meeting her at obscure places to avoid the paparazzi?

Or was he just hoping no one would see them out and about and realize they were together?

She had half a notion to decline the invitation. And if she hadn't had such a strong urge to see him again, she would have done just that. Instead, she said, "Okay, I'll meet you there." But her heart really wasn't in it.

Like Gram, didn't Amber deserve to be romanced, too?

Chapter Eight

While Jensen and Amber waited in the concession line
at the refurbished Golden Horseshoe Theater, he stood
like a young boy in a candy shop, studying the reprints
of old movie posters that lined the walls.

Could there be anything more perfect for a clandestine date, which wasn't supposed to be a date, than a
darkened cinema on a Wednesday evening?

And to top it off, *The Big Country* was playing tonight.

Sadly, at least for the proprietor, there weren't too
many people taking advantage of the low price and
1950s ambiance, but there was still a bit of a wait at
the concession stand.

Now, with his hand resting on the small of Amber's
back, his arm itching to circle around her, he didn't
care how long the lady in front of them took to place
her order.

When it was finally their turn, a young man in his late teens wearing a pair of black slacks, a white shirt and a red bow tie asked, "What can I get you?"

Jensen asked Amber, "What's your preference?"

"Something to drink—and maybe some munchies, like popcorn, I suppose."

"Very well then. We'll have a large buttered popcorn, a Kit Kat, a package of red licorice, those funny American sour candies shaped like naughty children and two large colas."

"Seriously?" she asked. "How long is this movie?"

"If I remember correctly, it's two hours and forty-five minutes, but it's one of the few long classics without a proper intermission, so I thought we should stock up."

The clerk tallied the order, and as Jensen paid the bill, it took only a moment to realize Mr. Murdock had received one hell of a senior discount. No wonder the proprietorship was able to get by charging such an inexpensive admission fee. They more than made up their loss on ticket sales here at the concession stand. Not that Jensen was complaining by any means. It was merely his habit as a financier to crunch the numbers and decide whether an establishment would succeed or not. Clearly, this place would do well on popcorn alone!

He reached for their refreshments and tried to balance one of the packs of candy and the popcorn container in his left hand, while grabbing his drink with the other.

Amber, proving herself to be quite practical, as usual, took the candy out of his hand and tossed it, along with the other packages, into her handbag before picking up her own cola and following him into the theater.

"Look, they have balcony seating," he said, not the least bit embarrassed about his excitement over the novelty.

"It seems kind of far away from the screen." Amber raised an eyebrow. "I don't think many people choose to sit in the nosebleed section these days."

"Come now. It's not that high. Besides, it'll be much more private up there."

When they settled into the velveteen upholstered seats, he took in all the details of the old-time cinema setting, feeling as though he'd traveled back in time to 1958, when the movie was first released.

The Gregory Peck and Jean Simmons film had been quite popular in Britain back in its day, and Jensen had seen it before on DVD and cable. But with the cinematography so up close and personal, the way the producers had originally intended, the experience couldn't be beat.

He glanced at Amber, who'd placed a red licorice stick in her mouth, her lips wrapped around it, taking it in...

Talk about new experiences. Being seated next to the beautiful and sexy Amber Rogers made it a bit difficult to keep his mind on the screen, especially when he was tempted to reach over and slip his hand in hers. But he forced himself to focus on the movie.

When Peck's character, sea captain James McKay, left New England, moved out west and fell in love with a wealthy cattleman's daughter, Jensen could relate to the man feeling like a fish out of water in a way he hadn't been able to before.

And when McKay dumped the spoiled Patricia in favor of the beautiful Julie, played by Jean Simmons, a funny burble welled up in his stomach—and it had nothing to do with the extra butter on the popcorn or the sugar high coursing through his bloodstream.

Hadn't he recently dumped the spoiled Monica, only to come to Texas and meet Amber...?

No, the similarity ended there. Everything was so much simpler in the movies, which was probably why he always found them to be such a pleasant escape from reality. But in the real world, men like him and James McKay had no business playing cowboys out west.

Yet, sometime during the course of the picture show, he'd succumbed to temptation and reached for Amber's hand. And while they sat in the intimate confines of the darkened balcony, he fought the growing urge to take her in his arms and promise her the world—or at least the water rights to a sprawling ranch. But he restrained himself, knowing they'd each have to return to their own lives soon. Their very different, very separate lives.

As the lights turned on and the curtain closed, he continued to sit in his seat, holding her hand, not breathing a word and trying to make the fantasy last for just a few more heartbeats.

Actually, he wasn't quite sure what fantasy he was trying to envision. Was he seriously entertaining the possibility that he and Amber might share something more than popcorn and candy at a movie?

"This was actually very nice," Amber said, interrupting what could surely be a dangerous line of thinking. But she didn't pull her hand away. And when she cast him a pretty smile, he felt as if he'd just won the UK National Lottery.

"I'm glad you enjoyed it." He glanced down at the empty popcorn bucket in her hands. "Hopefully, I didn't fill you up on too much junk food because I had my cousin Wendy set up something for us at her restaurant."

Amber glanced at her wristwatch. "But isn't the Hollows Cantina closed now?"

"Yes, it is. And that makes my surprise all the more special."

Her brow lifted again. Why was she so skeptical of anything he said?

"Are you going to cook for me?" she asked.

"No, not exactly. I've never been much of a chef. Why? Should I have prepared something for you myself?"

"No, of course not. I only…well, it's just that Elmer took Gram on a date yesterday. And they came here to the movie theater. Then he cooked her a fancy gourmet dinner. I was beginning to think that you were getting dating tips from Elmer Murdock."

Jensen laughed. "I can see why you might. And while Mr. Murdock is full of advice, some of which actually has merit, I came up with this one on my own. He merely mentioned the Golden Horseshoe, and I thought about bringing you here. But the dinner afterward was completely my idea."

She sighed with relief. "That does make me feel better."

"I must admit that some of my previous dates might wish that I sought out some dating tips from a real master, though."

The hint of a smile blessed her lips—pretty lips, full and kissable. "I don't buy that, Sir Jensen. The way the tabloids link you with a new starlet or supermodel every other month, it's obvious that the women clamor to be your next conquest."

He laughed as he escorted her out of the nearly empty theater. "Yes, one would get that impression. But don't believe everything you read and see. In reality, my work and family obligations keep me far too busy for much of a romantic life."

"Speaking of work," she said, as he opened the door to his truck for her, "tell me more about what you do."

Was she trying to change the subject on purpose because she wanted to discourage him from thinking about any possibility of a romance building between them? Maybe she was trying to remind him to stick to friendly and neutral topics.

He got in on the driver's side, started the truck and headed toward his cousin's restaurant, telling her about his job as a financier at Chesterfield Ltd. and what it entailed.

He knew his work probably sounded dull, especially when compared to the exciting life of a traveling rodeo star.

She listened, though, which one would expect from a polite woman, but she had to think that he was the biggest wanker with all his self-talk.

Was his life truly as mundane as it sounded?

They pulled up to the darkened restaurant. He parked, and they climbed out. When they reached the front door, he held it open for her, as the sounds of Linda Ronstadt filled the air.

"Well, it's not locked yet, so I guess that's a good sign." She gazed around the empty room.

There was a single table set, but everything else had been cleared away.

"I'm just on my way out," Wendy said by way of greeting. "There's a pan of beef enchiladas in the kitchen and the plates are in the warming drawer. Help yourself to anything behind the bar, and don't worry about cleaning up. The staff comes in early in the morning." Then she handed Jensen a key and kissed him on the cheek before rushing out the door.

As Amber looked around, Jensen cursed himself for allowing his cousin to go a little too over the top in staging a romantic dinner for them.

He hadn't been lying when he told Amber he wasn't the Casanova type and that he never took the time away from his work or his family to pursue serious relationships—other than a week or two with Monica, although their relationship hadn't lasted more than a few months, nor had it been serious enough to gain any special attention from the tabloids.

"Do you mean to tell me that you arranged for us to have the place to ourselves?" Amber asked.

"Well, I called Wendy and told her I owed you dinner and that we would be in the cinema until late. All of this wasn't completely my idea. Unless you think it's terribly impressive, in which case, it was one hundred percent my doing."

At that, she blessed him with a pretty smile, and his nervousness—Jensen was never ruffled around the ladies, so where had that come from?—soon dissipated.

"Can I get you a cocktail?" he asked. "Or maybe some wine?"

"A glass of merlot sounds good."

He went behind the bar, found a nice bottle of California wine and uncorked it. Then he carried it to the table and poured them each a glass.

Hopefully he hadn't laid it on too thick. He didn't want her thinking he was trying to seduce her, but at the same time, he had to wonder if deep down, maybe he was.

"I'll get our dinner."

As he turned toward the kitchen, she followed him. He should have known Amber wouldn't be the type of woman to merely sit still at the table like a regal queen, waiting for someone to serve her.

It was one of the things he liked most about her. She always seemed willing to jump in and lend a hand—to his sister, to her grandmother or to anyone who needed it.

After he filled their plates full of hot and cheesy enchiladas, they carried them back to the intimate table, where a small candle flickered in the votive.

Since he didn't want to give her the impression that he was trying to wine and dine her, he talked about the movie, horses and about anything else that would be considered neutral territory.

"I'm certainly going to miss the delicious southwestern food when I go back to London," he said as he finished his last bite.

She paused, fork in midair. "When are you leaving?"

She seemed surprised—as if he'd announced he was going tomorrow.

Would she miss him if he was to go so soon? Or would she be relieved? He knew she didn't like having her name linked with his in the tabloids.

"Not until after the weddings in February. I'm sure the whole town will be glad to see the lot of us go and take the sleazy paparazzi with us."

"Oh, I don't know about that. I think a few of the townspeople are enjoying the notoriety."

"Maybe. But some of them are just fame and fortune

seekers, looking for the opportunity to get a piece of the limelight. I can't stand people like that. If they had any idea how terribly difficult it is to go about their lives and protect their families from bloodthirsty newshounds stalking them every second, maybe they'd rethink that."

She shifted in her seat, and he wondered if his tirade had made her uncomfortable. He'd never been able to stomach the poor little rich boy image, either.

It wasn't as though he was trying to sell her on becoming a permanent fixture in his life, thank goodness. Because, if he was, he was sure making a jolly muck of it.

And as pleasant as the thought of having her become his temporary lover was, he knew better than that. The two of them were as different as night and day, as oil and water, as...

He glanced across the table at her, wondering if her thoughts had strayed in that direction, too. After all, they'd been tiptoeing around a temporary relationship of sorts—laughing and sharing, holding hands and kissing each other senseless.

The glimmer in her eyes, which had been glowing in the candlelight just moments ago, seemed to have dimmed—or perhaps that was merely his imagination.

If he had made a muddle of things, then perhaps that was just as well. Nothing could come of this—whatever this was. And the sooner he put that fool notion out of his head, the better.

So why couldn't he keep his gaze or his thoughts to himself?

Four days later, Amber entered the side door of the Horseback Hollow Grange Hall, carrying her saloon-girl costume on a coat hanger. Of course, no one knew exactly what it was, since she'd carefully draped a green plastic trash bag over it, hiding it from public view.

To be perfectly honest, she was beginning to have second thoughts about agreeing to show up for the stupid dance rehearsal/audition that Larry Byerly from casting had lined up for today. But after Gram had gone to so much trouble to make the ruffled dress, which was actually pretty darn good, she hadn't had the heart to consider changing her mind.

Besides, she'd been avoiding Jensen ever since their date at the Golden Horseshoe the other night, and moving toward a future without him seemed to be a good game plan—and one that would keep her heart from getting any more involved than it might otherwise be. The problem was, she was falling for the guy—like it or not—and could see heartache coming at her like a raging bull.

And though she had no business dancing the cancan, even in the privacy of her own bedroom, she'd agreed to come out today and accept some "private instruction" to see if she was "teachable." Even if she wasn't, they still wanted her to be the face on their ad campaign and planned to do a trial photo shoot today.

She thought the whole thing was just plain nuts, but she got a kick out of it, too. So she would listen to whatever they had to say.

Nothing like a little down-home notoriety, huh? But if there was something she knew deep in her soul about her fellow townspeople, it was that they were usually a forgiving lot—at least, with each other and when given time.

She knew she wouldn't be a complete dud today.

She'd done a little acting in high school and had twirled around in front of the mirror a lot as a kid. She really couldn't compete with a professional dancer, though.

Besides, riding in the Wild West Show was going to keep her busy enough. So she probably ought to tell Larry to forget it, to go find his local gal somewhere else since most of the townsfolk would be opposed to one of their own having anything to do with Cowboy Country USA.

It was just that she'd never liked people telling her what she should or shouldn't try out for. It only made her more determined to give it her best shot.

"Miss Rogers!" Larry called out. "It's good to see you. I was afraid you might not make it. Come and meet GiGi LaSalle, the choreographer. She'll work with you for twenty minutes, then we'll see how quickly you catch on. It's all very simple."

Yeah, right. She smiled and greeted GiGi, a tall, slender woman in her early thirties. "I...uh...brought a costume. Should I put it on?"

"By all means." Larry pointed toward the rear exit. "The ladies' room is down there."

Amber knew exactly where it was. She'd been coming to the Grange Hall for wedding receptions, family reunions and pancake breakfasts sponsored by the volunteer fire department since she was a kid.

"I'll be right back," she told him.

Moments later, she stood before the mirror, all decked out in the red-satin-and-black-lace ensemble Gram had created, her shoulders bare, her breasts more prominently displayed than she was used to. She tugged at the fabric, hoping to cover up a bit of the swell, to no avail.

She supposed the costume wasn't all that revealing, at least, by some people's standards. But while a lot of women liked showing off their wares, she usually kept her blouses buttoned nearly to the neck—other than that top she'd worn to Smokey Joe's. The one that Jensen seemed to think had caused every cowboy in the place to gawk at her.

Just the thought of his jealousy drew a smile to her lips, and she cocked her head to the side, assessing herself in a way she never had before.

Dressed in denim and cotton, she'd always thought of herself as just one of the cowboys—only a bit on the feminine side. But in red satin and lace, with every curve blatantly exposed one way or another, there was no doubt she was a female through and through—and pretty darn sexy, if she did say so herself.

"Miss Rogers?" Larry called out. "We don't have all day. I have other dancers coming in to audition—and we need to be out of here by six o'clock. The mayor's daughter is having her wedding rehearsal here tonight."

Amber quit her preening and exited the restroom, carrying her folded street clothes and boots with her.

"Oh, wow," Larry said. "I knew it. You were a natural."

She tugged at her neckline. "No, I'm not. I've never had a dance lesson in my life—other than this one."

"You're a natural in that costume. Who'll care if you flub up? Everyone will be watching you in that dress." He glanced at GiGi. "Don't you agree?"

"She definitely has potential, in a Podunk rodeo queen sort of style."

Who was GiGi calling Podunk?

She nearly objected when GiGi reached out and grasped a lock of her hair. "Do you mind?"

"Mind what?"

"If I just improve on what you're working with here. Larry, give me five minutes and be prepared to be wowed."

Amber sighed and gave a little shrug. Gram used to try to dress her up for Sunday school, especially at Easter and Christmas. But Amber usually threw such a fit, the poor woman gave up.

Doggone it, Gram had once said, *if the Good Lord knew how hard it was to get you ready to go to church, young lady, He'd tell me to stay home.*

GiGi walked to the corner of the room, where she had a multidrawer case of some kind. She brought it back and opened it up, revealing a wide display of makeup and things a Hollywood hairstylist might need.

A few minutes later, she'd whipped out some blush, lipstick, eye shadow and mascara and made quick work of applying it to Amber's face. Next, she teased Amber's hair to new heights, then whipped it into a twist or topknot of some kind. "Now go take a look at yourself and tell me what you think."

She thought GiGi and Larry were a couple of over-the-top wannabe stage parents, but she kept her thoughts to herself and returned to the ladies' room. When she glanced into the floor-length mirror, her breath caught.

Wowzer. She looked va-va-voom sexy now. Mae West could eat her heart out. But more to the point, what would Jensen say if he saw her in it?

It was sure to turn his blue blood raging red-hot.

Of course, she didn't look as if she was in the twenty-first century anymore—or in Horseback Hollow, for that matter. But the look Larry and GiGi had been going for was definitely accomplished.

She almost hurried to the corner where she'd left her belongings so she could grab her cell phone out of her purse and take a selfie to show Gram, but she didn't want to come across as a complete country bumpkin.

Oh, well.

For the next twenty minutes, GiGi showed her some moves. She wasn't a complete klutz, and while it took her some time to get it right, she finally caught on and had a few laughs in the process.

After the audition, Larry explained the idea behind Madame LaRue's Lone Star Review. "We'll have someone play the piano, there'll be a comedian, some actors will do a shoot 'em up at the bar. It'll be a nightly dinner show—and a real addition to Cowboy Country USA."

"I'm already committed to ride in the Wild West Show," Amber said. "My attorney looked over the contract, and I signed on. As fun as it could be, I still run a working ranch. And while I followed through on the audition because I told you I would, I won't have time to be involved in two productions. So you're going to have to find another cancan dancer."

"All right, I understand. But speaking of attorneys…" Larry looked at the young assistant sitting on the folding metal chair and taking notes. "Remind me to talk to the suits about making an addendum to Miss Rogers's contract…"

"Why would you do that?" Amber asked.   •

"After what we've seen today, we're gonna need to add a clause about you being our local PR gal. As far as the dinner show goes, we'll have plenty of saloon girls to perform, but since we plan on having you as the face on the posters, we'll need you to make some appearances."

"I'm not sure I even want to do one appearance." She glanced at her wristwatch. "Listen, I need to take off."

"No problem. We have the next auditioner in the ladies' room. Thanks so much for coming. We'll have our photographer get in touch with you for the upcoming publicity shoot."

"Like I said, we'll need to talk about that later." Amber still only planned to commit to the Wild West Show, although she actually liked the idea of having her photo in the ad, especially dressed in costume.

She snatched up her clothes from the spot on the floor where she'd left them. But rather than stick around long enough to change back into her jeans and shirt, she decided to head home dressed as she was. Besides, she hadn't taken that selfie, and she wanted Gram to see her all dolled up, with her hair and makeup done.

She could hardly wait to see the look on her grandmother's face.

But it wasn't just Gram who'd get a gander at Amber after GiGi and her magic makeup box had their way with her. When she arrived at the ranch, she found a couple of unexpected vehicles parked in the yard. The first was Elmer's green machine, which she supposed shouldn't have been all that surprising. She couldn't say the same for the other one, though, which was Quinn Drummond's pickup, the one Jensen had been using.

Evidently the handsome Brit had decided to stop by unannounced, which was fine with Amber. But from the look on Jensen's face, the surprise was really on him.

While looking in the mirror of the Grange Hall restroom, she'd wondered what he would think if he was to see her in the saloon-girl getup. But in all her imagining, she hadn't been able to envision his actual expression when she climbed out of her truck dressed in red satin, her hair pulled up in that fancy twist GiGi had coiffed, her face painted, her shoulders bare and her breasts ready to burst out of the neckline.

And poor Jensen looked a bit stunned, to say the least. You'd think he didn't know whether he was afoot or on horseback.

Chapter Nine

When Amber climbed out of the ranch pickup dressed like she'd just stepped off the back lot of a Wild West movie set, she could have knocked Jensen over with a feather boa—if she'd been wearing one. And that seemed to be the only thing missing.

She smiled as she closed the driver's door. "Cat got your tongue?"

Apparently, more than his tongue was missing. His brain had been nabbed along with it.

"What's the matter?" A grin tickled her lips. "You're looking at me as though you think I've been out on the town, throwing down whiskey shots and dancing on the bar of every beer joint in the county. Haven't you ever seen a saloon-girl costume before?"

Yes, but she'd caught him completely off guard, and he'd be darned if he knew what to say.

"Have you been driving around town dressed like that?" he asked, hating the jealousy that found its way into his voice.

At that, her grin faded. "No, I just came back from the Grange Hall."

"What, pray tell, were you doing out in public dressed like that?"

She crossed her arms, which thrust her breasts upward—and nearly out of the outfit completely. "Is this some kind of inquisition?"

"No, I'm sorry. It wasn't meant to be. It's just that…" He scanned the length of her, from the upswept hair and—blimey. Had her eyes always been so large, her lashes so thick? And those cherry-red lips…

His imagination, along with his hormones, was running amok. And while he'd never considered himself a jealous man, he didn't like the idea of her running around town so…so exposed.

"Did you stop by for a reason?"

Actually, he had. He'd noticed a breach in paparazzi security at the ranch and thought he'd slip away to see her in person, to ask if she'd like to ride into Vicker's Corners to spend some time together. He hadn't given the details much thought yet, but he wouldn't be opposed to taking her for an ice cream cone and some window-shopping or some other perfectly simple and innocent venture.

He'd been going stir-crazy inside his sister's house, and if he had to look at Quinn and Amelia gushing all over each other anymore, he'd take a polo mallet to the first camera lens he might encounter upon his escape. Luckily, though, he hadn't had to take extreme measures to slip away.

But seeing Amber dressed like one of the vixens of the Wild West, he was no longer thinking of ice cream or considering a date that would end up being either simple or innocent.

"I came by to see you," he admitted. "Just to talk, or to maybe whisk you away for a bit. But seeing you dressed like that—stunning and beautiful... Well, you've just shot my original plan all to hell. And now I'd like to whisk you away all right. But to live out a cowboy's romantic fantasy."

She glanced down at the dress, and his gaze followed, continuing down her shapely legs. *Damn.* It had to be the most grievous of sins to keep limbs like that covered in denim.

"The folks down at Cowboy Country USA were looking for a local girl to be in their ad campaign. They also..." She paused, glanced at her bare feet, which made him wonder what shoes she'd been sporting earlier. "Well, they had some other coals in the fire, which is what Larry Byerly had been talking to me about the other night at the Hollows Cantina. So Gram stitched up this costume for me, and I met him and another fellow at the Grange Hall earlier. It was all fun and games on my part. Sort of. I probably should have changed before I came home, but—"

"I'm glad you didn't."

They stood like that for a moment, in the waning light of dusk—the beautiful saloon girl and the...

What? Who was he, really? A British royal—or a polished, stuffed toff?

Right this minute, though, it seemed that the only answer that really mattered was the one Amber could give him. And as the silence enveloped them, the layers of his facade—some gold, perhaps most gilded, but all of them carefully erected over the years or maybe even the centuries—seemed to slowly peel away.

The sounds and scents of the Texas ranch in the evening set an interesting stage for an intriguing fantasy that was building by the minute. And in spite of his social standing, his upbringing and his better judgment—which he couldn't seem to fall back upon—a question rolled out of his mouth. "Is there someplace where we can be alone?"

Amber gazed at him with soulful eyes, and as she did, something passed between them—although he'd be damned if he knew what it was, since he'd never experienced the like.

"Gram and Elmer are in the house," she said, "but there is somewhere close by where we can talk in private, although it's not suitable for royalty."

"I'm not royalty. I'm just…Jensen."

And tonight, that's exactly who he was.

Amber took his hand and led him to the barn. Once inside, she turned on the light. "There's no one around to see us in here—other than the horses. And I can assure you that they won't gossip or take photo ops."

"That's a relief." He led her over to a hay bale, and they took a seat. But once they did, things turned awkward.

When he'd mentioned getting her alone, he hadn't meant to sit and talk. And doing any more than that in a barn…well, it just didn't need contemplating.

He had no idea what to say, other than how utterly beautiful she was—and how just looking at her gave him an out-of-body experience. Bloody hell, it was an out-of-this-century experience, as well.

To get things back on an even keel, he said, "I'm not sure how much longer I'll be in Horseback Hollow. My mother wants me to stay until after the weddings in February, but I have business obligations back home."

"Yes, you said that the other night. Is that what you came to tell me?" she asked.

"No, it's not." Perhaps he should be honest. "I came because I thoroughly enjoy being with you. I lo—I like your wit, your sense of humor, your spunk. And you've made my time in Horseback Hollow most pleasant."

"Pleasant? I hope that's more complimentary in London than I'm taking it about now."

"I'm sorry for the language barrier we seem to have, but yes, I find myself thinking of you at all times of the day and night. And when I do, those thoughts make me smile."

"I'm glad to hear that, Jensen, because I feel the same way. When I first met you at Quinn's house the day after Christmas, I didn't like you. And I thought we'd have issues if we ever met again. But I actually like tangling with you."

He laughed. "Tangling, huh?"

"Yep."

They sat there for a moment, side by side on the hay. Then he reached out, took her hand and felt the work-roughened palm he'd come to admire.

"Is that why you wanted to be alone? So you could tell me that?"

He pondered the wisdom of pure honesty, but only for a moment. The lack of pretense was what he liked best about his relationship with Amber. And yes, it had become more than a friendship lately, although he wasn't entirely sure how much more.

"Actually," he admitted, "I wanted us to be alone so I could tell you that I wouldn't mind..."

He'd never been at a loss for words with women before, but this was different. Amber was different. And not in the most obvious of ways.

"You wouldn't mind what?" she asked.

Now it was his turn to grin. "Tangling with you tonight."

At that, she turned to him, her lips parting. "You want to argue and banter?"

"No, not at all. I didn't mean sparring verbally." He brushed a kiss across her lips—lightly, tentatively. "There are other ways to tangle. Like this."

"When put that way, I'd be agreeable to tangling with you." She broke into a pretty grin, transforming the saloon girl into a... Hell, he wasn't sure what, exactly, but princess certainly came to mind.

"This barn wouldn't be conducive to what I'd actually had in mind," he said, "but if you give me a little time, I'll plan a romantic evening. That is, if you don't mind a temporary fling with a man who finds you an amazing, intriguing and delightful woman."

With that, she gave his hand a squeeze. "I'm up for a temporary tangle, even though I'm not into one-night stands or casual affairs. But I've come to care for you, Jensen. And because we live in different worlds, there doesn't seem to be any other way for us to see where our kisses might lead."

"So you'd be okay with a no-strings attached affair?"

"To be honest, if you leave town and I never see you again, I'd always regret not knowing what we might have shared—even if it's just a one-time thing."

"Then I'll find us a perfect romantic getaway."

"No need to do that. I have one available—right here, right now."

In a dirty, dusty barn? Surely she wasn't serious.

But when she placed her hand on his cheek, he realized that she was indeed serious. And with that gentle touch, the slight roughness of her palm uncovered a raw desire that sent his hormones soaring and his blood racing, and he realized he'd agree to anything she suggested.

"Come with me." She stood and took his hand, walking toward a ladder that led to the hayloft.

As Amber led Jensen up the steps, as he watched the sway of her hips, he was glad that he'd thought to bring a condom with him. Not that he planned to have need of one tonight, but he didn't take chances. And he'd... well, he'd hoped something like this would happen, although he'd never expected to have a saloon girl suggest that they make love in a hayloft.

Still, he found the whole idea rather exciting.

When they reached the top rung, he couldn't believe what he saw. Several quilts had been spread over the hay-littered flooring near a rickety nightstand that held a battery-operated lantern and a portable radio.

For a moment, he had to wonder if she'd been expecting him and had planned to invite him to join her here all along.

"I haven't been up here in a year or longer," Amber said, "so it might be a little dusty. But it's comfy."

Rodeo posters of cowgirls lined the walls, and a small bookshelf held several paperbacks and a stack of magazines.

"This was my hideout when I was a teenager. I used to come up here to read and think. And often just to dream." She shrugged, then strode over to the night-stand and turned on the lantern, as well as the radio, which played the sounds of soft rock. "It might not seem like much to you, but it was a castle in a faraway land to me back then."

"It looks pretty special to me now."

And so did she.

As they stood in the hayloft, in the yellowed glow of the old lamp, he felt rather heroic, like a Western sheriff who'd fought the bad guys and returned to town after earning the right to woo his lady's heart.

Her heart? All daydreaming aside, their reality didn't allow him the luxury of assessing the emotions involved, although admittedly they were brewing under the surface.

But right now, all he could think about was how lovely and alluring Amber was, dressed in that sexy red satin and looking at him as though she was feeling every bit as aroused and tempted as he was.

He reached out and unpinned her hair, allowing it to fall along her bare shoulders and down her back. She smiled, then scooped her soft curls aside and turned so he could unzip her costume. He took a moment to linger, to inhale her peach blossom scent and to graze his fingers along her skin.

Finally, he reached for the zipper. As the garment opened and slipped to the ground, she turned to face him wearing a black strapless bra and matching panties. His breath caught. The cowgirl had morphed into a goddess, a sight to behold.

Her body, curvaceous yet lithe, was everything he'd imagined it to be and more.

Talk about fantasies coming to fruition. But for the life of him, this was one fantasy he never wanted to end.

As Jensen drew Amber back into his arms and claimed her with a heated kiss, she leaned into him, ready to give him all she had to offer—and to take whatever he was willing to give.

If the kisses they'd shared had been a sample of what was to come, making love with Jensen was going to be magical—memorable. Yet it wasn't just a sexual act. Not as far as she was concerned.

He ran his hand along the curve of her back and down the slope of her hips, then pulled her hips forward, against his erection, letting her know how badly he wanted her. A surge of desire shot clear to her core, and she pressed back against him, revealing her own need.

When she thought she was going to die from the ache of her arousal, she ended the kiss long enough to un-snap her bra and let it drop to the straw-covered floor.

"I knew you were beautiful under that denim and flannel, but I had no idea you were so…stunning, so perfect." He reached for her breasts, his thumbs skimming her nipples and sending her senses reeling.

She knew better than to think about concepts like forever when they only had tonight—or perhaps a few more like this. But everything about Jensen and what they were doing seemed so right.

When she feared her knees would no longer hold her up, he scooped her in his arms and carried her to the quilt. Then he dropped to one knee and gently lay her down. A true knight—with or without the official royal title.

He studied her for a moment, passion glazing his

eyes, then he proceeded to remove his shirt, baring himself to her. When he was undressed, and she caught the full sight of him, the sheer beauty of his chiseled chest and abs, she scolded herself for ever thinking polo wasn't a serious sport. The man was well-muscled perfection, and she wanted to pull him down to her so they could start kissing right where they'd left off.

"I hope you don't think I came here planning to do this tonight, but I did bring some protection along with me."

"If I'd known this was going to happen, I would have had fresh linen, rose petals and candles."

"I'm glad you didn't think of candles. I can't imagine how we would have explained a barn fire, especially if the news reached the *Cross Town Crier.*"

She laughed. "And then the paparazzi would have had a real heyday with that."

"They might have said our scorching hot affair had set the quilt on fire."

"Think we should risk it?" she asked.

"I might spontaneously combust if we don't."

She laughed, then opened her arms. He joined her, and they continued to kiss, to taste, to stroke each other, skin to skin. As her thumb brushed across his nipple, he sucked in a breath.

For a moment, her feminine confidence, which had been soaring through the roof only moments ago, waffled. "I'm sorry my hands aren't as soft as the other women you've—"

He grabbed her by the wrists and gave them a firm squeeze, his gaze locking on hers with an intensity that stilled her voice, her thoughts and even her fears. "Your skin and hands are perfect, Amber. And your work ethic is one of the things I find most attractive about you. Don't ever apologize for that. Your touch stimulates me in a way I've never experienced."

"You aren't just pulling my leg?"

His expression softened, and a smile tugged at his lips. "I meant what I said about tangling with you earlier, so I might tug your legs a bit before the evening is over. But all translations aside, your hands are exquisite."

Then he kissed all her insecurities away until she was drowning in need. After he slipped on the condom, he entered her. And as her body responded to his, as their tempo increased until there was no one else in the world but the two of them, it seemed that they were in that magical castle she'd always imagined this old barn to be.

This wasn't Amber's first time making love, but it certainly felt like it. Jensen was an amazing lover—no doubt experienced with all the "dalliances" she'd read about, the women he'd dated all over the world.

But she wouldn't think about that now. Not while he was doing such amazing things, making her body move and arch, releasing far more than an uninhibited sexuality she hadn't realized she had. He was triggering emotions she'd only dreamed of feeling.

As his tempo increased, she raised her hips to meet him, feeling as though she was on a sexual roller coaster, her heart racing, her pulse spiking. She went up and up, then raced down and around.

She was in and out of control, yet breathlessly anticipating each and every unexpected jolt and turn. And as she reached a peak, she cried out and let go. Jensen shuddered with his release, and they came together in an earth-rumbling, soul-soaring climax she would never forget.

As she held him close, enjoying the ebb and flow of the most amazing afterglow, she was reluctant to release her hold because making love with Jensen had been a ride to beat all rides.

And since she'd just come to realize that she didn't want to settle for a temporary affair, this was one carnival ride that was bound to break her heart in the end.

Jensen didn't dare breathe, let alone move.

He wasn't anywhere near as sexually experienced as the tabloids reported him to be, but he'd certainly been with worldly women before—and in some rather glamorous locations, including five-star hotel suites, Scottish castles and more than one Italian villa. So needless to say, a Texas barn was a first.

But if he was to compare making love with Amber in a hayloft to the rest, the other ladies and bedrooms would pale.

Whether in denim and flannel or red satin and black lace, Amber Rogers had a way of rocking his world. And in this case, she'd certainly pulled the proverbial rug out from under his feet.

Not to take Texas colloquialisms too far, but how in blue blazes had she done that?

The mutual desire had been a large part of it, sure. When she'd cried out with her climax, he'd released with her in a sexual explosion that had him seeing stars, in spite of the fact that they weren't out in the open and that there was an old wooden roof overhead.

He rolled to the side, yet he continued to hold her

close, reluctant to let her go. He didn't have to ask how it was for her. He'd felt it in her touch, heard it in her sighs.

They lay like that for the longest time, sated and… well, amazed was a pretty good description.

He feared the questions that might follow, things like, Where shall we go from here?

Because, in reality, whatever they'd shared this evening couldn't really go anywhere other than here in Horseback Hollow. As fond as he'd grown of Amber, as much as he'd like to spend every waking hour he had with her while he was in town, he couldn't see them having much more than that.

Their lives were so completely different that it would be impossible to mesh them. Besides, he had family obligations in London and a patriarchal image to maintain.

He could, of course, come visit her from time to time, whenever he was in town to see his family. But he couldn't expect her to put her life on hold, staying single for those few and far between visits.

Still, as he drew her close, as he inhaled her faint peach scent and pulled a piece of straw from her silky hair, he felt as though he held an unexpected treasure.

Amber Rogers was an attractive and intriguing woman, one he found entertaining and a world apart from the upper-class socialites he normally dated. She also made him smile as often as she challenged him, which kept him on his toes.

Not a day went by, and hardly a moment, that he didn't think about her and wonder what she was doing. They'd become close friends, dear friends. And now they were even more than that—they were lovers.

Of course, as soon as the weddings were over in February, he'd be making a trip to the airfield, where he would board a chartered flight on Redmond-Fortune Air to Dallas, connecting to British Airways and flying first class to Heathrow.

But for the first time since in arriving in Texas, Jensen wasn't the least bit homesick for London—or eager to return.

Chapter Ten

Jensen refused to risk Amber's reputation with the threat of the paparazzi still lurking. And even if he wasn't concerned about them making a tabloid-newsworthy spectacle of themselves, he couldn't trust himself to see her and keep his hands off her. Instead, they talked on the mobile several times each day. But it was never enough.

He'd give anything to whisk her away to a deserted island, where he could be alone with her, but they were stuck in Horseback Hollow, where he was finding it more and more difficult to keep their relationship quiet. All his efforts at secrecy made him fidgety—or maybe his wish to spend every spare moment he had with Amber was doing that.

Either way, Quinn had picked up on it and brought it to the forefront during the third week in January, while they had their morning coffee.

"Looks to me like you have a little cabin fever," Quinn said.

Jensen slipped his hands into his trouser pockets, and his fingers wrapped around the gold watch. "A bit, I suppose. I can't seem to slip out of here without the paparazzi sitting up and taking note."

"You sure that's all it is?"

No, but Jensen didn't feel like talking about it. "They'll eventually get tired of hanging out here and go look for a story elsewhere."

"Seems like you'd be used to all that. There's nothing else bothering you?"

"Being away from home for so long has me concerned about the office, the Chesterfield estate and that sort of thing."

"That's it, huh?"

"What makes you think there's anything more than that?"

"Because you're wearing out the floorboards pacing back and forth. And you keep picking up your cell phone—or mobile, as you call it—as if you're dying to place a call. Yet I know what time you typically talk to your assistant back home, thanks to the time change, and that you told me that your office seems to have things well under control across the pond." Quinn took a sip of coffee, stretched out his legs and smiled. "So I thought it might have more to do with a pretty former rodeo queen."

Jensen stiffened, but he didn't give his brother-in-law's theory any credence. At least, not verbally. Ostensibly, his body language might not be so subtle.

"I'm the last one in the world to believe anything

those tabloids print," Quinn added. "But I have to admit, you look a little lovesick to me."

"That's ridiculous."

"You'd know best," Quinn said.

"That's right." But did he really?

Jensen blew out a sigh. "All right, I'll admit it. Amber Rogers has caught my eye—and she's taken up a good deal of my thoughts. But nothing can come of it. And while I'd like to spend more of my time with her while I'm here, I don't want her to have to deal with the paparazzi."

"I hear you. Those jerks made Amelia's life hell for a while—mine, too. And we've been keeping a low profile so they won't do it again." Quinn carried his empty mug to the sink and rinsed it out. "But if you and Amber enjoy each other's company, it seems a shame to let those guys ruin what little time you have left."

He certainly had a point.

After Quinn left the kitchen through the mudroom, grabbed his hat and headed outside, Jensen sat alone, pondering his dilemma. He'd let his worries about his privacy and the paparazzi steal precious time he could have spent with Amber face-to-face. And the clock was ticking. He only had about three weeks left in town.

Who knew when he'd be back? So he reached for his mobile and called Amber.

She answered on the second ring. "Good morning. You're up early."

No need to tell her he hadn't had a full night's sleep since he'd left her ranch the night they'd made love in her barn. "I thought I'd have a cup of coffee with Quinn."

"What? Trading in your teapot for a coffee grinder?"

She tsked her tongue. "Sounds as though the Texas ruffians are having a bad influence on you."

"You may be right." Jensen found himself leaning back in his chair and grinning, as carefree as a child with no responsibilities in the world. "I was wondering if you'd like to go out to dinner with me tonight."

"You already paid off your wager."

"I was talking about a date—a real one."

"Seriously?"

"Yes. And if you have something other than blue jeans, you might want to dress up a bit."

"Like a saloon girl?"

Jensen laughed. "As much as I'd love to see you in that sexy red dress again—in a barn setting or in the privacy of my bedroom—you'd better leave the costume at home."

"All right. Just tell me what time and where to meet, and I'll be there."

They agreed upon seven o'clock at The Garden in Vicker's Corners, and then Jensen set about making plans for the evening.

He was leery of being caught with Amber for more reasons than one. The paparazzi would have a field day with it—The Prince and the Cowgirl… Or, heavens! What if they'd gotten wind of her in that sexy saloon-girl outfit?

Still, Amber was worth the risk of a little notoriety, especially if that meant spending some quality time with her.

That evening, as Jensen prepared to leave for his date with Amber, his mother was seated on the divan at the Drummonds' ranch, her mobile in hand, her head bowed.

"What are you doing, Mum?"

Lady Josephine glanced up, her cheeks flushed. "Sending a text."

Where in the world had she ever learned how to send texts? One of Toby's kids must have taught her. The oldest boy loved anything electronic.

His mother was one of the most technologically challenged people he knew, although it was high time she joined the rest of the world.

She slipped her mobile into the pocket of her tailored slacks, assessed him with a mother's eye and smiled. "My, don't you look handsome. Where are you going?"

"Out for the evening."

"Where? And with whom?"

"I thought I'd take Amber to dinner in Vicker's Corners."

"That sounds lovely." His mum stood and walked over to fix the collar of his Western shirt.

And yes, Jensen was cautiously dipping into Horseback Hollow fashion in an effort to blend in with the locals and draw less attention.

Mum cocked her head to the side. "Are the two of you…?"

"No, not at all." The last thing he needed was for his mother to worry that she'd lost another one of her children, especially the one who'd taken the helm of the family finances and assumed a patriarchal role, to the Texas countryside. "We're really just friends."

"Oh."

"No need to give the tabloids any more fodder for their silly stories," Jensen added, as he took in the quiet cleanliness of the living room. Little Clemmie was sleeping in the bassinet, and his mum had prepared a quiet, romantic dinner for Quinn and Amelia in the kitchen.

Then he noted that she'd combed her hair and freshened her makeup. "So what are you up to this evening? Are you going back to Aunt Jeanne Marie's house?"

"Yes, but Gabriella is hosting a small dinner party for her brothers, Cisco and Matteo, at Jude's ranch this evening, and I've been invited. So I'll be going there first."

Gabriella, Orlando Mendoza's daughter, was engaged to marry Jude Fortune Jones, Jeanne Marie and Deke's son. They were just one of the couples who would be married in the big wedding ceremony that would take place on Valentine's Day.

"Gabriella wanted me to bring you along, and I thought that you could take me. But if you have plans…" His mum trailed off, as though she hadn't expected Jensen to have anything else to do in such a small town.

"I'd be more than happy to drop you off," he said. "It's on the way. And since you've been staying with Jeanne Marie and Deke, you can ride home with them."

"Splendid." She brightened. "Let me just grab my pocketbook."

Fifteen minutes later, Jensen was helping his mother up into Quinn's pickup. Was it his imagination or had she sprayed on some extra perfume?

Not that he noticed those things usually, but she had seemed to take an inordinate amount of time to grab her purse. She must really be missing the London social scene if she was primping this much for a simple dinner party in Horseback Hollow.

"You look lovely," he told her as he started the engine.

She smiled. "Well, I want to make a good impression on the Mendoza family." Her mobile buzzed and she pulled it out, checked the screen, then giggled.

Had his reserved mother actually erupted in childish pleasure? What were Toby's kids up to?

He could ask, he supposed, but he wasn't the type to pry into other people's text conversations. So he continued to drive, thinking about his date with Amber. While he was looking forward to wining and dining her—in a way she deserved—he needed to keep in mind that the two of them were little more than friends, no matter how entertaining he found her.

Or how amazing he'd found their lovemaking.

The sooner he steered his mind in a different direction, the better. He had family obligations, responsibilities, and his life was a world away from Texas.

"Are you getting eager to return to England soon?" he asked his mum.

He knew she liked being close to her daughter, her new grandbaby and her newfound sister's family. But Lady Josephine Fortune Chesterfield was more British than the parliament building.

"I miss being home on the Chesterfield estate, but this funny little town is starting to feel like a second home. In fact, I was thinking of possibly speaking with a real estate agent about purchasing property here."

"Truly?" he asked, completely gobsmacked.

"Not to live full-time, of course. But I plan to visit Amelia and that sweet little Clemmie often. I don't want to be a thorn in their side, always staying at their house. Besides, if I do purchase a home here, it will give you, Lucie and your brothers a place to stay when you come to visit."

"I can't imagine either Oliver or Brodie spending much time in this tiny Texas town."

"Perhaps not. But I would have said the same thing about you a few weeks ago, and you seem to be getting along splendidly here."

Jensen had to admit that he'd enjoyed his time here. But he also had a business and clients to get back to. He couldn't stay out here playing cowboy indefinitely.

But when he thought about saying good-bye to Amber and not seeing her until his next visit to the States, something tightened in his chest.

They had certainly developed some type of connection, but not one that could withstand half a continent and an entire ocean.

Their worlds were too far apart—and not just physically.

He was a noble, a gentleman, not a ranch hand. And she was a rodeo queen, not a lady of the realm. There was no way they could forge a lasting relationship. They were simply too different.

It was better for them to just enjoy each other's company for the time being and not think about what the future most certainly did not hold for them.

"You know, Orlando's sons are single," his mom said as they pulled into the driveway at Jude's ranch.

"Hmm," Jensen murmured, not quite processing his mother's line of conversation.

"It must be so nice for him to have his family now living nearby. Perhaps his sons will find wives soon and settle down in Horseback Hollow permanently."

"It seems to be the common thing to do lately."

"You know, Amber Rogers is single and lives locally.

Perhaps you should mention the Mendoza boys to her. Perhaps, we can introduce them."

"Amber? *My* Amber?"

"Oh, I didn't understand her to be *your* Amber." Lady Josephine smiled, that knowing smirk she often displayed when she'd caught her husband sneaking biscuits or scones to one of the children before dinner time.

"I didn't mean she belonged to me," Jensen said. "Quite the contrary, in fact. But she has quite a bit going on in her life right now. Running her family ranch keeps her busy. So I'm sure she isn't in the market for a new beau."

Or was she? She'd seemed eager enough to consider romance when Jensen had taken her in his arms.

He'd like to think that was because he had instilled that passion in her. But what if it wasn't him? What if she was lonely, and he just happened to come along at the right time?

Still, she wasn't some young woman making her first appearance at a debutante ball in order to snag a husband. And he should know. He'd been to plenty of them—and he knew the look of a woman on the prowl for a husband. Amber Rogers definitely did not fit the bill.

Yet, long after he dropped his mother off at Jude's ranch, her suggestion lodged itself into his mind and he couldn't dislodge it. He'd even been tempted to go inside and meet these Mendoza boys just to confirm that they weren't possibly Amber's type.

But he was already running late. So he'd only walked Lady Josephine to the door. And before he could be invited inside, he'd dashed off.

It wasn't jealousy that had made him leave so suddenly. He was in a hurry to get to the restaurant and reassure himself that his date couldn't possibly be interested in dating anyone else.

He'd never been the possessive type, but he was determined that as long as he remained in town, he would be the only man with whom Amber would spend her time. After that, he wouldn't allow himself to think of her marriage options.

Maybe it was selfish, but he wanted her all to himself. Which was why, when he arrived at the restaurant before her, he again asked the hostess to seat them in a quiet, out-of-the-way corner.

The Garden in Vicker's Corner was a trendy bistro with stained-glass windows, copper ceiling tiles and a vintage art-nouveau crystal French chandelier in the entryway. Despite Amber's travels to some of the bigger cities throughout the great state of Texas during her short-lived rodeo days, she'd never been inside a restaurant this fancy.

"I've heard how great this place is," she said. "People need reservations weeks in advance to get in. How long have you been planning for us to have dinner here?"

Jensen chuckled, then lowered his mouth to her ear. "Not long at all. Despite the need to be on the lookout for constant media hounds and social climbers, wealth and notoriety also comes with some advantages."

Amber stopped soaking in the decor long enough to lift a brow at him. The way "social climbers" had rolled out of his mouth had put a sudden bad taste in hers.

She suspected that gold diggers and people wanting to move up in class and status often tried to take advantage of him, so he'd had to put up an emotional barrier to keep them from getting too close. But now that he was becoming firmly entrenched in their sweet little Texas town, who would he suspect was attempting to climb his social ladder?

Certainly not her. But ever since that night in the hayloft, she felt a little uncertain about where things stood between them. So she found herself reading into everything he said. She'd have to stop doing that.

"I can see where having financial and social advantages would come in handy for you in London Town, but how does that work for you here in Vicker's Corners?"

"You'd be surprised what you can do with some of those green advantages you Americans have—the kind with pictures of your old presidents and patriots on them. I've found them to be quite helpful in making my stay here in Texas a bit more pleasant."

The maître d' himself, a middle-aged man who'd introduced himself as Roland, led them back to a white linen–draped table for two, which was once again in a secluded corner. A single red rose in a bud vase, as well as a flickering candle in a votive, provided a romantic ambiance.

After Roland handed them menus and made sure they had ice water with lemon slices and a basket of fresh bread, he left them alone.

Still, Amber lowered her voice. "So you bribed someone to get us reservations?"

"I wouldn't call it a bribe. It was more like a sizable contribution to ensure our privacy and to enhance our dining experience."

She liked having him to herself. It also gave her an opportunity to get to know him better. So she reached for a slice of pumpernickel and asked, "What was it like to grow up in England? Did you have a happy childhood?"

"Brodie and Oliver, my older half brothers, may have had it a bit differently before my mum married my father. But I've never heard them complain. So I think they'd agree that we all had the very best of childhoods. We grew up on the Chesterfield estate in England."

"I can't imagine what that might have been like. I suppose you had tons of servants."

"It wasn't like that." Jensen took a sip of water. "Mum wasn't a traditional mother by aristocratic standards."

"What do you mean?"

"She didn't hire nannies to raise her children. She did have help, but she was in complete charge of the nursery, as well as the household. Our family may have been titled and privileged, but she was determined that we wouldn't take our money or royal station for granted."

Amber leaned her arms on the table, eager to hear more, yet not wanting to break the spell Jensen cast upon her when he finally began to open up about himself. So she sat quietly, but attentively, waiting for him to continue.

That is, until the sommelier interrupted him. "May I interest you in one of our wines, sir?"

Once Jensen placed their order for a bottle of zinfandel from California's Napa Valley, Amber steered him back toward the conversation she meant to have.

"So you didn't grow up with a house full of servants?"

"Quite the contrary. We had plenty of them, but they were under strict orders to ensure we weren't spoiled rotten."

The sommelier returned with the red wine, removed the cork and let Jensen have a sample. "It's fine. Thank you."

After filling their glasses half-full, he left them alone again.

"I was an only child," she said. "So I find this fascinating."

Actually, she found Jensen fascinating—and not just the way the candlelight glistened in his hair, the way he held his wine goblet, turning it just so and studying the deep, burgundy-red color. And she was thrilled that he'd finally begun to open up to her.

"After Brodie and Oliver went off to school," he said, "my mother was busy with Charles and the girls, so my father would take me to the stables with him. We spent a great deal of time together, he and I. And as soon as I learned basic arithmetic, he had me adding up his ledger books. He told me never to trust anyone else with the family business or finances. I guess I took it all a little too much to heart."

"How so?" she asked, taking the first sip of her California wine.

"I was always a stickler for the rules. Charles used to tease me and try to get me to lighten up, but the sense of family responsibility had been engrained early on."

He sounded as though he'd been the perfect son, the perfect child.

"I'll bet your teachers loved you," she said.

"They did. I was the one they would send on special errands. In fact, I was a prefect my second year at Eton."

"A *prefect*?"

"It's a student who's put in charge of the others."

"Like an associated student body president?"

Jensen furrowed his brow. "I'm not sure."

Maybe she shouldn't make too many comparisons to their school systems. She didn't want him losing focus.

"So you went to Eton? Even I've heard of that. Where did you go for college?"

"For university you mean? I went to St. Andrews in Scotland, naturally."

Naturally. "Did you always do what your family expected of you?"

He picked up his goblet and swirled the wine in the candlelight, his expression growing wistful. "Father used to say that he could count on me for anything. I mean, he was close to all of his children and loved us all equally. But even Mum will tell you that Father and I shared a special bond. We enjoyed the same things like polo, managing finances, being with our families— even watching old cowboy movies."

"I would have liked to have met him."

Jensen reached into his pocket for a moment, then withdrew his hand. "My father and I even shared a love of airplanes, although he was a pilot and I wasn't."

"Did you ever think of taking flying lessons?"

"Occasionally. But now that he's gone, I think about it even more. What I'd really like to do is purchase a jet. That way, I could visit my family in Texas whenever the fancy struck."

"Seriously?"

Again, he reached into his pocket. "Well, I'll probably take those flying lessons. And I might even buy a jet. But I'd hire the pilots."

She lifted her linen napkin, trying to hide the smile that touched her lips. If he flew here regularly, she'd get to see him more often. But she didn't want to corner him into making promises out of an offhand comment, so instead she said, "You keep reaching into your pocket. Why is that?"

"Oh." He pulled out an antique gold watch. "This was my father's, and his father's before him. It's silly really, but whenever I think about him, I have a habit of toying with it."

"That's sweet. How did he pass?"

His expression dimmed, and for a moment, she thought he might change the subject, but he looked up from the treasured heirloom and continued. "He died of a massive coronary while playing polo four years ago—almost to the day. The family was devastated."

Amber thought of Pop's death, what his loss had meant to her and how she'd given up her rodeo career in order to return to the ranch to be with Gram and to help her through it.

"I'm sorry," she said.

"So am I. It wasn't easy to step in and take over the helm of the family holdings and investments—but not because I couldn't handle it. My father had trained me well, and I was already doing much of that when he died. The difficult part was that I suffered more than just the loss of my father and the family patriarch. I lost my best friend and confidant."

The grief he still carried after four years was etched deeply in his face, and her heart went out to him.

"I suspect that you handled it all with grace—and that you did your best to take care of everyone else."

"My father would have expected it. And my mother needed me to be strong."

"Did you have anyone to lean on at the time?"

What she was really asking was if he had a girlfriend

or a significant other in his life. But even though it had come out innocently and seemed like a natural question to ask, she knew better and winced at her inappropriate curiosity, especially at a time when he was sharing his heart.

It was just that she'd like to have a small part of his heart—if he'd only give it to her.

"I started to talk to my mum about it one day," he admitted, "but she was so heartbroken herself, I couldn't burden her with my grief."

"What about friends or…someone else?" There she went again, probably sounding like an insecure teenager, prying about the other women in his life when she ought to wait for a more opportune time.

But Amber would have given anything to be the one who'd comforted him back then, the one he could have opened up to.

"I realize the tabloids all seem to say that I'm one of England's most eligible bachelors. And while I do attend plenty of social events and usually have a lady on my arm, that's merely an image I project."

"I can't believe women aren't clamoring to date you," she said, a green twinge of jealousy rising up inside.

"Perhaps they are. But my life isn't as glamorous as it seems."

The life he lived didn't seem the least bit glamorous to her—not if he didn't love her back and she couldn't be a part of it.

"Every time I appear in public with a woman, the gossip columns predict a wedding. And if I go on my own, without a date, they wax poetic about why I won't commit."

"That must be aggravating."

"It is. I'm very careful about what I do and the image I project—just as my father was. I wouldn't do anything to soil the family name. But I've learned to take those tabloid headlines in stride. I'm stronger than my sister Amelia in that respect. She went through terrible turmoil last spring when they falsely announced her engagement to Lord James Banning. So don't believe everything you read."

She leaned back in her chair, somewhat comforted. "So no ladies back home are spitting nails because you showed up in the tabloids kissing a Texas cowgirl?"

"Absolutely not. I wouldn't have done what we did the other night if I was involved with anyone that way."

Of course he wouldn't. Amber would expect nothing less of the prim and proper Jensen, but it still felt good to hear him say it out loud.

"So what about you?" he asked, changing the subject. "Did it hurt to give up the rodeo?"

"I told my grandmother that I'd grown tired of the traveling and being away from home. But Gram is my only family. And I didn't want her to think I'd sacrificed my dreams to be with her while she grieved."

The maître d' came by to take their orders—the prime rib for him and the herb chicken and red potatoes for her.

She assumed the topic of their conversation would change, but after he left, Jensen asked, "Why the rodeo?"

"Because I'm good at it, for one thing. But I also did it for Pop. My dad used to compete, which tickled him to no end. But when he married my mom, she thought bronc riding was too dangerous. So he gave it up, moved to Houston and got an office job. After my dad died, she couldn't support me on her own. So she moved home to the Broken R."

"Then you took up barrel racing?"

She smiled. "I couldn't ride broncs, but it was a way to compete in the rodeo—and to make my pop proud."

"From what I heard, you were a natural."

"That's what Pop said."

"So you just gave it up? Just like that?"

She bit down on her bottom lip. She could probably let it slip now—at least some of it. "Yes, I gave it up, but I have an opportunity to ride again. Not in the rodeo, but as part of the Cowboy Country USA Wild West Show."

He stiffened, and she wished she had kept it to herself. Heck, she'd implied that the whole thing was still under consideration. What would he say or do if he knew she was already committed?

The maître d' came by with their salads, and the conversation stalled for a while.

She'd been prepared for a gradual change of subject, but not for the silence that followed. But maybe Jensen was just being introspective.

"Does that bother you that I might ride in the Wild West Show?" she asked.

"Of course not. It sounds like a reasonable compromise."

Did it?

Maybe she should give him some time to chew on it before she told him that she was not only committed, but legally bound.

When their dinner was served, they made small talk while they ate. But the sooner it came time for the bill to be paid and for them to go their own ways, the more

Amber's stomach rebelled at the roasted red potatoes and the herb chicken.

She'd give anything to take Jensen home with her or to drive off to a place where they could be alone, but it looked as though they'd be getting into separate vehicles again tonight.

Even after what they'd shared in the loft.

Her stomach knotted, and she pushed her plate aside even though it was still laden with enough leftover to take home for lunch tomorrow.

Finally, she lifted her goblet and took a sip of wine, preparing to bolster her courage.

"It's a shame nothing can come of a relationship between the two of us," she said, hoping and praying he'd tell her she was wrong.

Jensen reached out and placed his hand over hers, enveloping her with warmth. "As much as I'd like to argue, I can't see how it could."

In spite of the fact that she'd known all along that they'd never have a life together, Jensen's words drove a spike in Amber's heart dead center, creating a crack that threatened to break it in two.

Still, as long as he remained in town, she was determined to spend as much quality time with him as she could.

Because when he left Texas, he'd made it clear that the only part of his life she could claim wouldn't be his future.

It would be his past.

Chapter Eleven

Under normal circumstances, if Amber had heard her grandmother say that she was going on an overnight trip with a single man, she would have been shocked speechless. But when Gram casually mentioned over breakfast that she planned to accompany Elmer on a two-day trip to Lubbock for a reunion with his military buddies, Amber didn't raise a protest or voice a judgment.

Well, she did nearly choke on her coffee. But when she'd finally coughed it into the correct passageway, she decided not to look a gift horse in the mouth.

Having the ranch house to herself meant that she and Jensen could finally have a private place to meet and have the talk she'd been wanting to have since their dinner at The Garden, and she was going to use the opportunity to its fullest advantage.

Once the older couple took off in Elmer's car, their

names branded on the back window, Amber reached for the telephone and, while butterflies swarmed in her tummy, placed the call she'd been dying to make all morning.

Jensen answered his cell on the second ring.

She'd barely greeted him when she blurted out, "What would you say if I told you I had the house to myself for the next two days?"

"Are you suggesting you'd like company tonight?"

"Yes. And not in the hayloft this time."

"That sounds wonderful. I'd offer to cook you a romantic meal, but as we discussed before, my culinary expertise is somewhat limited."

So was Amber's, but she didn't need to advertise that fact. Besides, she had plenty of other skills to make up for it.

"Should we meet at the Hollows Cantina?" he asked. "I've had a craving for carne asada."

"Another private dinner?" she asked. Because if that's what he wanted, they could order takeout and bring it back to the ranch.

"No, I think it's time we dined in the main part of the restaurant with everyone else."

What? No more clandestine meetings? As much as she looked forward to having the house to themselves later tonight, she was glad to know that he didn't want to keep her—or their relationship, if that's what it was— under wraps anymore. And she counted that as a good sign. A very good one.

Evidently they'd reached a turning point. Maybe it was time to level with him about Cowboy Country USA. She could tell him that she'd decided to fully commit to the Wild West Show, although she wouldn't mention anything else. First she'd gauge his reaction to the trick riding.

When the call ended, Amber set about getting ready for the weekend by changing her bedding, setting out scented candles in her room and choosing some romantic CDs to have ready for Jensen's arrival later that night.

Then she took the last two hours to fuss with her appearance—taking a bubble bath, doing her hair and choosing just the right outfit to wear. There'd be no jeans or flannel this evening.

Now, as she looked at herself in the full-length mirror, she studied the low neck of her silky top, one she'd gotten as a gift but had never worn. She wondered if she'd gone a little overboard. After all, it wasn't as if she and Jensen were meeting at a fancy restaurant out of town or in a dark movie theater.

They were going to the most popular restaurant in town—and on a Friday night. Everyone would see them together and, with her decked out in such obvious dating attire...well, it would pretty much be a coming-out party.

She glanced at the swell of flesh peeking out between the low swoop of her blouse. She hoped she'd chosen something that was enticing enough to remind Jensen of what she had planned for the rest of the evening, but not risqué enough to make her look like a truck-stop floozy.

When she had spent as much time as she dared, she reached for the perfume she favored but rarely used and applied a dab, wondering if Jensen would appreciate her efforts.

Or would he want her to cover up? The straitlaced

Brit sure seemed to have a bit of a jealous side. Or had she read him wrong?

He hadn't seemed to mind flaunting other women on his arm. So why her? Was it jealousy or embarrassment?

She shook off the insecurity. Either way, when she told him about Cowboy Country USA, she wouldn't mention the part about the ad campaign. It didn't take a crystal ball to know how the proper gentleman would feel about that, especially if the press got wind of it.

But even though Jensen would be long gone by the time Amber had to start posing for photographs in that saloon-girl costume, she'd keep that little secret to herself.

She took one last glance at herself in her mirror.

The clock was ticking. And she wasn't just talking about this evening and the need to stop primping so she could get on the road.

In a few short weeks Jensen would be leaving for London. And who knew how many more times they'd have to spend together?

For that reason, she would pull out all the stops tonight.

Jensen arrived at the Hollows Cantina before Amber and cursed the bloody paparazzi for his reluctance to pick her up and take her on a proper date.

Rachel Robinson, the hostess, greeted him and asked if he would prefer his usual table in the back corner. But Jensen had decided not to keep Amber or their relationship hidden anymore.

Besides, after the knowing smile Quinn had flashed at him when he'd handed him the car keys, their secret was bound to get out eventually. And maybe, somewhere deep inside, Jensen actually wanted it to. So he'd told Rachel to reserve the table in the middle of restaurant and headed to the bar to wait for Amber.

He'd just placed a drink order when a cowboy turned toward the entrance, broke into a broad grin and gave a slow wolf whistle. Several other men at the bar, along with Jensen, followed his gaze and spotted Amber sashaying into the cantina.

The slinky black blouse she wore wasn't any less revealing than that damn saloon-girl costume. And her jeans fit her like a pair of denim gloves, leaving very little to the imagination when it came to those shapely, not-so-hidden legs underneath.

He stood, fighting the red-hot pulse at the side of his neck. He told himself that the mooning cowpokes in this place were used to seeing Amber dressed in working clothes and that they were merely surprised by the change in her appearance. But the woman was as sexy as she was unpredictable, and he was tempted to whisk her away to someplace private—and not just so he could keep her hidden, but so he could have her all to himself.

She spotted him straightaway because she headed for the bar.

"Hello," she said as she slid onto the stool he pulled out for her.

As if just now realizing that everyone—even the women who'd gathered in the bar—were studying the two of them, she asked, "What're they staring at?"

"You, my dear." From where he stood, he had a clear vantage point of the swell of her breasts, which he'd caressed a few nights before. And he forced himself to look away for fear his words would stall in his throat.

She ran a hand through her glossy hair, as though

taming her long and loose locks could downplay how magnificent she looked. "Am I overdressed?"

"Not at all. You're stunning." He took his seat and handed her the margarita he'd ordered for her—the exact one she'd been drinking the night she'd come with Mr. Murdock and her grandmother.

She looked at the delicate silver-and-turquoise watch on her wrist. "Are they still having the two-for-one happy hour special?"

Did she think he was a tightwad? He'd only been humoring Mr. Murdock before.

"I have no idea what time it is—or if there are any specials. I just thought this was your drink of preference. Did I get it wrong?"

"No, this is fine." She took a sip. "In fact, it's just what I need to calm my nerves."

"Amber Rogers? Nerves? I can't believe the fastest rider and best shot in Horseback Hollow, if not all of Texas, would be nervous about anything."

Did it have anything to do with being seen with him? Did the paparazzi unnerve her, like they'd done to Amelia?

Of course. She probably didn't want her friends and neighbors to know that they were sexually involved. After all, she'd told him she didn't have brief affairs.

And he couldn't blame her for feeling uneasy about it. Even if he was free of familial obligations and they didn't have a geographical barrier, he wasn't sure if he was ready to pursue her in the way his heart and hormones were urging him to.

Amazing. That was the closest he'd come to admitting that he actually cared for her, that he felt more than friendship and that his heart had become invested. And while he wasn't quite ready to broach the subject in public, he might do that later tonight, while they were alone.

Just as he lifted his drink to take another sip, a slick-looking gentleman, who looked more out of place in Horseback Hollow than Jensen felt, approached.

"Why, there's our pretty Amber. It's sure nice to see a friendly face in these parts." The man, who was in his late forties, ran a pinky-ringed hand between his fleshy neck and his collar.

If he'd had a camera, Jensen might have thought he was a paparazzo.

Amber, who seemed a bit surprised by the intrusion, turned to Jensen. "This is Max Dunstan, Jensen. He's with Cowboy Country USA."

Dunstan held out his thick, well-manicured hand while running a head-to-toe assessment of Jensen.

The men had barely made the customary greeting when Dunstan pulled out a seat and plopped down on the stool next to Amber.

Her eyes grew wide, and she glanced around the bar as though trying to determine whether any of the locals had noticed that she was hobnobbing with the enemy.

Jensen was an outsider, so his opinion about the whole Cowboy Country USA controversy didn't count for much. Nevertheless, while he liked the quaint appeal of Horseback Hollow, he also found the Wild Bill Hickok and Annie Oakley thing a bit intriguing.

In fact, as Dunstan delivered his fancy Hollywood talk, Jensen tuned out so he could take in the not-so-subtle looks being cast their way.

Amber shuffled in her seat a couple of times, as if she wanted to be anywhere but next to Dunstan. Jensen found the whole thing quite amusing—until he heard the words *photo shoot*.

He spun back around just in time to hear Dunstan ask Amber if she would bring the saloon-girl costume with her for the ad campaign.

"What ad campaign?" Jensen asked. "And what photo shoot?"

"Our Amber here," Dunstan said, "is going to be the face of Cowboy Country USA. Forget about princesses and Kate Middleton. When we're done with our publicity launch, little girls all around the world are going to want to be cowgirls just like Amber Rogers."

"What do you mean 'saloon-girl costume'?" Jensen asked Amber. "I thought you were only talking about doing some trick riding. And that you hadn't made any decisions yet."

"I planned to talk to you about that later tonight," she said, rather sheepishly.

"Whoops." Dunstan guffawed. "Did I spill the beans?"

Amber shot him a scowl.

"Sorry about that." Dunstan raised his hands in mock surrender. "When I saw the expensive suit and Armani shoes, I figured he was your lawyer and already knew about your contract."

What contract? Why did Jensen feel as though he'd just walked into a movie theater, only to find that he'd missed the integral opening scene?

Using his best "lord of the manor" voice, Jensen said, "No, I'm not her solicitor. I can assure you I'm more to her than that."

"No kidding?" Dunstan raised his brows and looked first at Amber, then at Jensen. "My bad. I didn't expect a saucy cowgirl like Amber to have a stiff suit as a boy-friend. No offense, buddy."

Buddy? Didn't this guy know who Jensen was? And who in the bloody hell was he calling a stiff suit?

"Thanks for stopping by," Amber said. "You have yourself a great night, Mr. Dunstan." Then she waved him off, dismissing him as graciously as Queen Eliza-beth would have expelled a naughty dog from the throne room.

As Dunstan walked away, she tipped her shot glass of tequila to her lips as if it were a porcelain cup of Earl Grey.

Yet something told Jensen that she was unsettled by the whole encounter.

Well, he was more than unsettled. He was down-right perturbed—especially at being kept in the dark.

"It sounds as though your gig with Cowboy Country USA is all but a done deal." He'd tried to tamp down the accusatory tone of his voice, but without much success.

"I was going to tell you about the contract tonight."

"Tell me what? That they offered you one? Or tell me that you signed one?"

"That I signed one."

"But I thought you were just going to ride in their pretend cowboy show. I didn't know about the dancing-girl business or the photos and publicity."

He hadn't meant to sound so petulant, like a child who didn't get a sticky bun for supper. She didn't owe him an explanation. But for some damn reason, he still hurt like hell—way down deep. And the thought of her parading around in some skimpy costume, modeling for photographers and seeking the limelight was the exact thing that he'd spent his life avoiding.

"This wasn't the way I'd wanted to tell you, but I don't need your permission or approval anyway." She straightened her spine, and he realized she was no longer embarrassed or worried about what the locals were thinking. Or him, for that matter. "When you go back to London, I'm going to stay here in Horseback Hollow and go on with my life the way I see fit."

"I didn't know that performing in a trashy, two-bit saloon-girl costume was on the top of your list for life achievements."

"First of all, it's not trashy. Gram sewed that for me. And second of all, I *like* performing. Not necessarily in a skimpy dress, but on a horse and in an arena. I miss the rodeo and I miss the thrill of riding. I'm not going to apologize for that."

"Nobody is asking you to apologize." He wished she would lower her voice. They were making a scene, and he hated the way the patrons were now looking at him as if he'd insulted one of their own. "I guess I was just taken by surprise. I didn't realize you were into all that celebrity rubbish like the others. I thought I knew... Oh, never mind."

"What did you think you knew? *Me?*" She gave a little snort. "Because if you really knew me, you'd know that I'm not doing this for any other reasons than the ones I already mentioned. The last thing I want is to be a celebrity living out my life publicly on the front page of every gossip magazine. But I guess you have that British nose stuck too far up in the air to see that life is more than hiding out in your sister's house and dating all the wrong people, just so the world will see you the way you want it to—and not the way you really are."

She reached into her purse and pulled out a few bills,

leaving them on the bar, before she got to her feet. "That should cover the cost of my drink. I wouldn't want you to add gold digger or moocher to the list of unflattering qualities you think I possess."

With that, Amber turned around and stormed out of the cantina.

Jensen reached into his pocket, removed the watch and glanced at it. He wasn't sure what had happened, but he'd certainly made a damn mess of everything.

Well, what had Amber expected—a profession of undying love and unconditional acceptance? It took all she had not to burst into tears before she reached the dark and safe confines of her pickup.

Of course she looked like some sort of fame-hungry celebrity wannabe. She could see why someone like Jensen, who'd spent his entire life avoiding the cameras, wouldn't want his precious family name linked with the new face of Cowboy Country USA. But that didn't make her a bad person or somehow beneath him.

But then again, she had no one to blame but herself. She knew where this relationship was going—nowhere. And she'd known that all along.

The two of them were like night and day. Their worlds and their paths never should have crossed.

Still, she'd let herself fall in love with Jensen in spite of all that. And her heart ached at the loss of something and someone she'd never stood a chance of having. She needed to have a good cry, but she'd be darned if she'd do it in the parking lot of the town's most popular eatery.

So she started the truck and drove home, her anger soon replaced with tears and self-recriminations.

When she arrived at the darkened ranch house, she

tried not to look at the romantic staging she'd carefully set up before leaving for dinner—the scented candles that would remain unlit and the Keith Urban CD that would remain unplayed.

Instead, she undressed and climbed into bed, where the soft and clean sheets had been scented with lilac.

She punched her pillow about ten times before succumbing to heart-wrenching tears and crying herself to sleep. But even then, she spent a fretful night, tossing and turning until dawn.

The next day, a cold sense of loss nearly swept her away when she woke at daybreak, alone in a double bed and in an empty house.

She showered and dressed in her work clothes, hoping that would help put a sense of normalcy back into her life. Then she went to the kitchen and put on a pot of coffee.

When her cell phone rang, her heart leaped in her chest. Hope rose, chasing away her sadness. Let it be Jensen, calling to apologize or at least to make amends.

Without taking time to check the number on the lit display, she slid her finger across the screen and answered.

"Hello, dear. This is Josephine Fortune Chesterfield." Amber nearly dropped her coffee mug.

What could Jensen's mother possibly want? Was she calling to gently reprimand Amber for engaging her son in a horrible public display of a lover's quarrel last night?

"I'm sorry to trouble you this morning, but I was hoping you might know where I could find Jensen."

"Not here," Amber blurted out, embarrassed that the royal English aristocrat would think her son had spent the night with her. Of course, if Mr. Dunstan would have just kept his big mouth shut, that's exactly what would've happened.

"What I meant," she explained to Lady Josephine, "was that he didn't sleep with me. I mean, he didn't stay here last night. In fact, I haven't seen him since I left him at the Hollows Cantina."

"Of course not, dear. I'm sorry for assuming otherwise. It's just that he left in Quinn's truck yesterday. But it's back this morning, and one of the horses is gone. Several of the men have ridden out on the trails and haven't seen him. I thought that, maybe, he'd ridden out to your ranch to visit you."

Was Jensen missing? Had he pulled a disappearing act?

"No, he's not here. Does he normally just up and vanish like this?"

"Jensen? Hardly. He's a very reliable person and conscientious. But I'm afraid today's the anniversary of his father's death. And with all the recent developments and changes in the family, Jensen is taking it rather hard this year."

Had his grief been complicating matters?

Of course it had, and Amber had neglected to realize how quiet he'd become after talking about his father's death, how keen he'd felt the loss of the man who'd also been his friend.

She poured out her coffee and placed the mug in the sink. "Don't worry, Lady Josephine. I'll find him."

She just hoped she would be able to keep that promise.

After ending the call, she headed to the barn. If Jensen was on horseback, her best bet to find him would be with Lady Sybil.

But before she could saddle her horse, the brass buckle in the bridle caught her eye, making her think of Jensen's treasured gold pocket watch.

Where would he go if he wanted to be close to his father?

The answer came to her instantly and she ran back toward the house and grabbed the truck keys off the hook in the mudroom.

She drove down the highway much faster than was reasonable. Just before she could pull into the small parking lot at the airfield, she caught a glimpse of a horse and rider at the southern edge of the fence.

She slowed to a stop nearly a hundred yards away, not wanting to startle Trail Blazer, the gelding she'd sold Quinn, or Jensen, who was sitting in the saddle, staring at the small planes parked near the runway. She shut off the ignition and climbed from the truck.

"Hey," she said softly, as she approached.

Jensen glanced over his shoulder. "Hello."

"There's a posse out looking for you, cowboy."

He shrugged a single shoulder. If the dark circles under his eyes were any indication, she'd guess that he'd slept just as badly as she had.

"I'm sorry," he finally said.

"It's okay. We all need to get away and clear our heads once in a while, especially on days like today, when we're missing a loved one. Let me just call your mom and let her know she can call off the search party."

"While I'm sorry for worrying everyone this morning, I was actually apologizing to you for what I said to you at dinner."

She paused, her cell phone in her hand. She probably ought to backpedal about now, quit while she was ahead. But she couldn't help it. She'd fallen for the handsome Brit, and she couldn't roll over and consider their relationship dead in the water before it even got off the ground.

"I said some mean things, too," she admitted. "Cowgirls are tough and they're stubborn. And to make matters worse, I don't like it when someone says I can't or shouldn't do something. I was going to apologize for not telling you about that Cowboy Country USA contract sooner, but then, when I saw your reaction, I got my dander up and, well…I didn't mean to cause such a big scene."

"What you said made sense. I need to stop hiding and start living my life. I'm going to head back to England for a while."

He was leaving? Already? "What about the weddings?"

"I might come back for them. I haven't worked everything out yet."

"Will I see you again?" she asked, not really wanting to hear the answer.

"I don't honestly know. I thought I knew who I was and what I wanted, but then I met you and my whole world was turned upside down. I thought we could have a simple and uncomplicated affair, but that didn't work out so well."

It had worked out nicely the one night they'd spent in the barn. And if they'd had a chance to be together more…

"I'm not like the rest of my family," he said. "I'm not made for a long-term relationship."

Amber bit her lip to keep from protesting. And she blinked to keep from crying. "Did your parents set the bar too high? Are you afraid you won't find what they found?"

"Actually, it's quite the opposite. I don't want to find what they found. Watching my mum grieve for her best friend and soul mate has made me leery of loving someone that deeply. I started to feel much more than I should for you, and then things got tricky. You weren't the only one making a scene last night. I can't believe that I turned into such a jealous and possessive arse, especially when I thought of all those men seeing you in your showgirl costume."

"Well, the costume is a bit much. When Mr. Dunstan said that every little girl would want to dress up as a cowgirl just like me, it made me realize that no parent would want to see their daughter wear a saloon-girl costume. So I plan to make some stipulations in my PR contract. I won't agree to their PR photo shoot unless they agree to let me wear something much more practical for horseback riding."

"Even if you wanted to wear that costume—which is quite beautiful, by the way, so my apologies to your gram for what I said last night—I had no right to imply you shouldn't wear it. My parents never tried to keep me from doing anything I wanted to do. And I shouldn't try to limit you, either."

"But you cared enough to try. Isn't that a good sign?"

"My misplaced jealousy is beside the point. It's better if we end things now. There's a reason I don't let women get too close. If I were to allow myself to fall in love with you and then I lost you, the pain would be devastating. And it might never go away. I can't risk it. I *won't* risk it."

She wanted to object, to argue. But she wasn't about to grovel. Not when he'd already convinced himself that things were over between them.

No, there was nothing Amber could do or say that would change his mind. And while she should be thankful that she could evoke that kind of emotion in him, it only made her pain and her sadness worse.

"Have a safe trip," she murmured before heading back to her truck.

He'd made it sound so simple—and, in a way, so had she. But letting him go without a fight was the hardest thing she'd ever had to do.

She would forever grieve for him and for what they could have had—if they hadn't been so different.

Chapter Twelve

Two days later, Amber couldn't stand it any longer. She needed some answers—and she needed them now.

Had Jensen gone home to London?

Had he stayed?

Her curiosity was eating her from the inside out, and she was dying to talk to him. But she didn't want him to think she was stalking him—or that she'd resorted to begging like a lovesick puppy.

So who should she quiz? Jeanne Marie? That seemed like a more logical choice than Lady Josephine because Amber couldn't very well discuss that sort of thing with his mother.

There was also Amelia. Hadn't his sister said that she thought Amber was good for Jensen and implied they'd make a perfect couple? Well, maybe not perfect. But she'd spotted something between them, just by looking at the photo of them kissing that had been plastered on the front page of the tabloid.

You're just what Jensen needs, Amelia had said at the hospital. *The camera caught a spark. And I've seen the banter between you. My brother hasn't lit up like that since before my father passed away. And even then... well, I think there's something going on.*

Right now, it seemed Amber's only ally was Amelia, so she whipped her cell phone out from her pocket and called the Drummond ranch. She told herself that if by chance Jensen answered, she'd hang up.

But she was in luck—Amelia said hello after several rings.

"Do you have a minute to chat?" Amber asked.

"Clemmie just went down for a nap, so, yes. This is a perfect time."

Amber filled her in—not about everything, of course. But she admitted that her attraction for Jensen had led to...well, there'd been no need to deny or hide her feelings at this point. She'd clearly fallen for the stuffy Brit who'd set her world on end, then jerked the rug right out from under her. And she told his sister as much.

"No wonder," Amelia said. "My brother is clearly confused. He hasn't been himself at all. I'm sure that's why he left."

"So he *did* go, then." He'd said he would, but she'd somehow hoped that he wouldn't, that he'd reconsider. He had, after all, admitted to having feelings for her.

"He'll return soon. I'm sure of it. And not just because of the weddings in February."

Amber wasn't so sure about that. Even Jensen had said he didn't know if he'd come back to see his cousins married. That would mean turning around and flying back across the pond again when the weddings were only a couple of weeks away.

"Thanks for taking time to talk to me."

"Call me anytime. And try not to be discouraged. Jensen will come around. We can always count on him doing the right thing, even if he doesn't know how right that thing is."

Amber didn't feel the least bit hopeful, but she tried not to let his sister sense her discouragement.

In truth, she was better off cutting her losses—no matter how badly her heart ached.

She and Jensen were too ill suited to make a match anyway. He was an uptight aristocrat. And she was going to star in the Wild West Show. She'd have to give up her dreams to live a life with him—although, she suspected that her competitive, cowgirl nature is what drew him to her in the first place. And while she might like to travel and see more of the world, she also loved Texas—and Horseback Hollow especially.

Yet, even if they could work out the geographical issues, there were still so many more differences. He hid from the paparazzi—at least, whenever he was with her. And she would make him front-page news.

No, it would never work out.

She'd be miserable. And so would he.

She deserved to fall in love with an American prince of a man, a real live Texan, a cowboy with roots in Horseback Hollow and not some faraway land where they butchered the English language and didn't appreciate sweet tea drunk from an ice-filled mason jar.

The next couple of days passed slowly. And in spite of Amber's resolve to put on her big-girl panties and get on with life, her cherished Horseback Hollow became a difficult place to be.

She'd avoided going into town whenever she could, but because Gram was often away from the house, spending more and more time with her new beau, running the household fell on Amber's shoulders. And today, they needed some groceries.

So she snatched her purse and the keys to the ranch pickup, then headed out the back door. She'd no more than crossed the yard when Gram and Elmer drove up, big band music blaring from the open window of his Dodge Charger and both of them grinning like teenagers.

"I'll see you later tonight," the retired marine said, as he dropped off her grandmother.

Gram blew him a kiss. "I'll have dinner ready when you get here."

Amber let out a sigh. She supposed she'd have to get used to having Elmer around. He was becoming a fixture, it seemed.

The green muscle car had no more than turned around and sped off, when Gram approached Amber with a big ol' smile plastered across her sweet, prim face.

"What's got you in such a happy mood?" Amber asked.

Gram lifted her left hand, which sported a sparkling diamond ring.

Seriously?

"You're engaged?" Amber asked. "To be *married*?"

"Yes, isn't it exciting? Elmer proposed this morning in front of everyone at The Grill, and I accepted."

Amber's shoulders slumped—and not just because

she thought Gram had tarnished Pop's memory by hooking up with Elmer Murdock. In truth, the sweet old coot had begun to grow on her. But that meant Gram would become a bride before Amber would—not that she'd ever been the kind to get all girly and dreamy over white lace, bouquets and promises.

Still, there was always a first time, she supposed.

"What's the matter?" Gram asked. "Aren't you the least bit happy for me?"

"I'm just a little surprised, that's all. I never expected you to get married again. And, if you did, I thought it would be to someone more like Pop."

"I loved your grandfather dearly," Gram said. "So don't get me wrong when I say this, but I gave up a lot when I married him."

Amber furrowed her brow. "What do you mean?"

"Come inside. I'll put on a pot of coffee, and we can talk."

Ten minutes later, as Amber and Gram sat at the antique oak table in the kitchen, their chat continued over two cups of fresh-brewed decaf.

"Your grandfather was a wonderful man and a good provider, but he was a quiet sort. And marriage to him meant that I had to give up my friends and the life I had in town when I moved to the ranch."

"I thought you liked the Broken R."

"I did—I do. And I never had any real complaints. But I used to have an active social life—something your grandfather didn't appreciate. He was never one for dancing or parties or even attending church socials."

"And so in waltzed Elmer Murdock."

Gram chuckled. "Jitterbugged was more like it. Elmer is always game to try something new or exciting. I know you probably think he's a little…wacky at times. But he's so funny, and he makes me laugh."

"I'm sorry, Gram. I hadn't realized how much he's added to your life. Or that you'd downplayed your own personality when you married Pop."

"It's not just that. On top of everything else, Elmer loves me, honey. And he tells me, which is something your grandfather had a difficult time voicing. What's more, I love him, too. I never expected to feel that zing again. And it's nice." Gram smiled, a spark lighting her eyes in a way Amber hadn't noticed before.

And it made her appreciate the man in a way she hadn't anticipated.

"Will you please give Elmer a chance?" Gram asked. "He'd do anything in the world for me. And for you, too."

Something told Amber that Gram was right about that. So how could she deny them her blessing? "Of course I will."

Gram wrapped her arms around Amber in a warm, loving embrace, which might have triggered an instant healing process if her heart wasn't so badly broken from her own lost chance at love. But Gram's happiness served as temporary balm.

Amber was beginning to realize soul mates came in all shapes and sizes. And one size didn't have to fit all.

At that moment, the telephone rang, interrupting their embrace.

"I'll get it," Amber said, before answering. "Hello?"

"It's Jeanne Marie, sweetie." By the chipper tone in her voice, she obviously didn't know that Amber had been left heartbroken by her British nephew. "How are you?"

"I'm fine." Amber used her brave voice—the one she took on right after she'd had a bad qualifying round. "How about you?"

"Busy with the big Valentine's Day weddings, of course. I was wondering if you'd be available to help us assemble the favors tomorrow."

Was there anyone in town *not* getting married? Amber didn't feel like celebrating the romances of four happy couples, but she couldn't very well say no. Besides, she'd be attending those weddings anyway. And maybe it would give her the opportunity to find out more about what was going on with Jensen. "Sure, I can help. Where are you doing it? And what time?"

"At my house tomorrow—about two o'clock."

"I'll be there." She just hoped she could keep a cheerful front while she worked.

"Wonderful. We haven't seen much of you, Amber. What are you up to?"

"Right this second? I'm heading to the Superette."

"And then what? Are you going back home?"

"That's the plan? Why?"

"Just wondered."

The woman certainly sounded upbeat. And inquisitive. Amber supposed organizing and maintaining strict schedules for four upcoming weddings would do that to a person.

Or maybe Amber was just being overly sensitive. A failed romance certainly sent a woman spiraling into the dumps.

They made small talk for a moment, then ended the call.

Amber continued on with her one errand of the day, but even a quick stop at the local market, where folks often got the scoop on what all the other locals were doing, nearly tore the broken heart right out of her.

Everyone she knew seemed to be having babies or getting married, and she couldn't wait to escape the local gathering place fast enough.

Then, to make matters worse, while she was standing in the checkout line, Mrs. Tierney, the owner of the market, put out the latest issue of the *Global Trotter*, the tabloid that had plastered the photo of her kissing Jensen on the front page several weeks ago.

"Congratulations," Mrs. Tierney said. "You must be over the moon. And I'll bet your grandmother is beside herself."

Amber glanced up from the cart she'd been emptying. "Excuse me?"

"On your engagement." Mrs. Tierney handed her the newspaper, with a bold headline that announced Sir Jensen to Wed His Cowgirl!

Amber would laugh if it wasn't so sad. She finally realized what Jensen had been talking about and how hard it was for people to live their lives—and their heartaches—in front of the paparazzi lenses.

She always thought rodeo girls had tough skin, but hers was newspaper-thin right now. Jensen had to be a robot to not let tabloid lies and rumors get to him.

Mrs. Tierney pointed to a photograph of a sparkling diamond ring—a huge rock, actually—that Jensen supposedly purchased for her and presented while on bended knee.

"I'm afraid there's no truth to that at all," Amber said, lifting her left hand, which was as bare as it could be. "See? No ring, no fiancé. No royal wedding for this cowgirl."

"That's a shame. I wonder who he bought the ring for?"

Amber didn't bother to even answer. Instead, she choked back the emotion and blinked backed her tears until her groceries had been tallied. Was that the business he'd rushed home to London to handle?

Had he been pulling one over on her with that whole never-want-to-risk-falling-in-love-and-losing-someone line? Because as much as the news rags embellished their articles, the picture didn't lie. The man on the front was definitely Jensen, and he was walking out of the Jewelry Shoppe carrying a small white bag.

Of course, he might have gotten his watch repaired.

The store telephone rang, and Mrs. Tierney put the caller on hold while Amber paid the bill. Then as Amber picked up her grocery bags and headed for the door, she refused to give into her sorrow or her suspicion about Jensen leading her on.

The new year had gotten off to one heck of a bad start, but she wasn't going to let it get the best of her. It didn't matter what Sir Jensen was doing back in England or who he was doing it with. Amber had so many new opportunities lined up and so much to look forward to. She lifted her head as she walked to the truck, determined to get right back up on the horse that had thrown her and to embrace a new attitude.

So instead of heading home, she drove to the Hollows Cantina, where she would have her very own belated "Auld Lang Syne"—and a mock toast to the new life she was determined to create for herself.

When Amber entered the Hollows Cantina, she was greeted by the hostess, Rachel. "Are you meeting someone for a late lunch?"

"Not this time. I'll just have a seat in the lounge. Thanks."

As Amber made her way toward the nearly empty bar, she thought she saw Rachel pick up the telephone and make a call, but she couldn't be sure. And what did it matter anyway? So she continued on, pulled out a stool and took a seat.

"What'll it be?" the bartender asked.

"I'd like a split of champagne, please."

"You got it."

She really wasn't a drinker—and the bubbly stuff tickled her nose—but she was determined to find something to celebrate, something positive to look forward to, something that would ease the ache in her heart or at least lighten her mood. And she didn't want another one of those dang Jose Cuervo–shot margaritas that Elmer and Jensen had always ordered for her.

She tapped the tips of her fingers against the top of the bar. First of all, there was her agreement to star in the Wild West Show. And since she no longer had to worry about what attention that might draw to the Fortune Chesterfield family, she could announce it from the rooftops.

Secondly, she'd played hardball with their corporate attorney, Max Dunstan, yesterday and had insisted that they drop the saloon-girl getup if they wanted to use her photograph in the Cowboy Country USA ad campaign, and he'd finally agreed.

"Well, I'll be," a male voice slurred from behind her. "Amber Sue Rogers. I haven't seen you since high school."

She glanced over her shoulder to see Brady Wilkins, the former Horseback Hollow running back who'd gone on to play a season at Oklahoma State University until a knee injury sidelined him for good.

"Hey," she said. "How's it going, Brady?"

"Not bad." He held a glass of amber liquid in his hand—no ice.

Whiskey, she guessed. Maybe bourbon. And from the smell on his too-close breath, it wasn't his first.

"Can I buy you a drink?" he asked.

"No, thanks. I just ordered."

"Want some company?"

Not really. She'd rather be alone.

And then do what? Mope and feel sorry for herself?

Before she could answer either way, he drew up the barstool next to hers and took a seat.

About that time, Marcos Mendoza walked in. He'd no more than glanced at Brady before speaking quietly to the bartender, who nodded. Then Marcos picked up his cell phone and sent out a text.

Brady slipped his arm around the back of Amber's barstool. "So how's it goin'? I heard you gave up the rodeo to come home after your grandpa passed. That's gotta be tough. I know what it's like to give up a dream, especially when you're good—like you and me were."

The bartender brought Amber's champagne, along with a chilled flute, and opened the split. "You okay, ma'am? Is this guy botherin' you?"

"Hell, no, I ain't botherin' her, Lester. Me an' her go way back."

The bartender eyed Amber carefully, letting her know all she had to do was say the word and he'd make sure Brady gave her some space. But she could take care of herself. "I'm okay."

"See?" Brady's hand slipped to her shoulder, and he

drew her closer, as though she'd agreed to be on more friendly terms when, in truth, they'd hardly said a word when passing each other in the hall during high school because they'd run in different crowds.

Funny how a drink and shared heartbreak made barroom buddies out of near strangers.

Footsteps sounded, and a camera flashed. Amber turned to the doorway, wondering who'd entered the bar. Her breath caught, and she nearly fell off her seat when she spotted Jensen stroll in wearing a black suit, a trail of paparazzi following behind him. And he was heading straight for her.

What the heck?

The cameras—at least four of them—continued to flash, but Jensen didn't blink. He bellied right up to the bar as if he was John Wayne himself, and snatched the only other empty seat next to hers.

Before the reporters could jot down Sir Jensen in a Love Triangle on their notepads, Jensen took her hand in his. "Unless you're caught up in a conversation with this cowboy, I'd like to have a word with you."

She'd been dying to talk to him since he'd flown home to London, but his surprise arrival had thrown her so off step, that she wasn't sure if she could wrap her mind around the words she'd been wanting to say. Yet she might not have another opportunity, so she'd better take him up on it. "Let's go into the back room where it's private."

"That won't be necessary." He glanced around the room. "Besides, I'm expecting an audience this time."

She followed his gaze, her jaw dropping when she spotted the people who'd begun to gather around— Gram and Elmer, their arms linked around each other and grinning from ear to ear. Jeanne Marie and Deke, along with Lady Josephine, her hands clasped together, as though waiting on bated breath for something...

Even Mrs. Tierney was here, but who was minding the Superette?

Rachel had wandered into the bar, too, along with Marcos and Wendy.

"What's this about?" Amber asked.

"I needed to talk to you, and I wanted it to be a surprise. So I asked Jeanne Marie to call your house and find out if you were home. She said you were heading to the Superette. I went looking for you there, but arrived too late. Mrs. Tierney said you went home, so I started back to the ranch, then Rachel called Amelia, and she told me you were here."

"How did Rachel know you were looking for me?" Amber asked.

"I suspect Wendy told her since news travels fast in the Fortune family. So I sent Marcos a text and asked him to hold you here, even if he had to hog-tie you."

Amber turned to the drunken former football player, then looked back at Jensen. "I don't suppose you asked Brady to waylay me."

"Not on a bet. Your cowboy friend might be harmless when inebriated, but I wouldn't trust my lady with a man who's not related to me."

"Your *lady*?"

"It's taken me a while to admit it—and a while longer to decide what to do about it. But you've become very special to me, Amber. And I want—no, I need you in my life."

"I didn't think you were coming back."

"The first thing I did when I arrived home was to

spend a little time at the cemetery so I could talk to my father. Just sitting there in the family plot, it became clear to me that I wasn't sparing myself any pain by walking away from you. I missed you so much in those few days I was gone that I couldn't stand it. Like I told you before I left, I was confused. And I had some things to think about."

"Did you?" she asked. "Get things worked out in your mind?"

"Almost. There's just one little bothersome question, but you can settle it for me." He reached into his lapel pocket, withdrew a small, black velvet box and dropped to one knee.

Then he flipped open the lid, revealing a stunning, sparkling diamond ring that looking amazingly similar to the one she'd seen in the most recent issue of the *Globe Trotter.* "I love you, Amber Rogers. Will you marry me?"

Cameras flashed from both sides of them, as people began to crowd around.

"Cat got your tongue?" he asked, a smile sliding across his face, as he used the same phrase on her that she'd once used on him.

"Are you sure about this?"

"Absolutely, positively certain."

She merely gaped at him, unable to believe what he was saying—what he was doing. And in front of an audience, no less.

His words and his sweet romantic gesture were being recorded for all the world to see—or read about in the tabloids.

"My old polo injury is starting to flare up. Are you

going to keep me down on my knees?" he asked. "Or do I have to grovel?"

"Oh, my gosh. I'm sorry, Jensen. I was just so taken aback. And speechless, I...Oh, for Pete's sake." Amber dropped to her own knees. Then she wrapped her arms around his neck. "I love you, too. And yes! I'll marry you. I have no idea what our life will be like together, but it will be a thousand times better than living apart."

Then she kissed him for all she was worth.

When they came up for air, the entire bar hooted and howled and whistled and clapped. Lady Josephine was the first to congratulate them, tears welling in her eyes. "I'm so happy for you two. I knew Jensen would eventually find true love—when the right woman came around."

Jensen stood and drew Amber to her feet. "It seems that I've found my soul mate, too, Mum. She isn't at all like you, but she's every bit as sweet and loving. She's not soft-spoken—and she can raise quite a ruckus when she wants to. But that's fine with me. I've come to enjoy, as my good friend Elmer Murdock would say, a little spit and vinegar."

Amber gave him a gentle punch in the arm. "Did you know that Gram and Elmer are going to be married?"

"Yes, he told me."

"Goodness, Jensen. Did everyone know you were coming back to town but me?"

"I wanted to surprise you."

"Even the tabloids knew. But I didn't believe them!"

"I saw that. The jeweler must have leaked a photograph of the ring. Apparently, that's one story they actually got right!"

"By the way," Lady Josephine said, "I have so much

to celebrate. Oliver is going to visit soon. He'd told me he was too busy to come, but apparently he's had second thoughts and wants to meet little Clemmie. So if you'll excuse me, I'm going to order some champagne for everyone here!"

"That's nice that Oliver is coming," Amber said. "I'll look forward to meeting him."

"I'd like to introduce you," Jensen said. "But something doesn't quite add up."

"What do you mean?"

"There might be more to the story than what he's told Mum. But I suppose we'll find out when he gets here."

Gram and Elmer were the next to congratulate them.

"I'm so happy for you, dear." Her grandmother leaned down and kissed her cheek. "I know that your young man will make you just as happy as Elmer has made me."

"Your grandmother has her heart set on a simple wedding at the courthouse," Elmer said as he, too, kissed Amber's cheek, then shook Jensen's hand. "But if you two have a mind to do one of those double ceremony thingies, I'm sure we can get us a twofer one special at the Grange Hall."

Amber's gaping stare must have conveyed her distress at the suggestion of a double wedding in a multipurpose venue because Jensen rushed in to save her from hurting the old man's feelings.

"Actually," Jensen said, "that's terribly kind of you to offer, Mr. Murdock, but since the town would have already experienced attending a quadruple wedding, I wouldn't want our special events to pale in comparison."

"I got you, son." Elmer winked at them. "Originality is important, especially to the little ladies. Forget about the dual wedding then. We'll just rent one of those jumbo RVs with the extra pop-out sides and do our honeymoons together."

"Lord help us," Amber murmured as Lady Josephine tried to distract Gram and Elmer from further suggestions. "So what about after the wedding and honeymoon," Amber asked Jensen. "Where will we go from there?" They still lived worlds apart.

"I wouldn't mind settling in Horseback Hollow," he said, "although I'd have to travel to London regularly."

"Seriously? That's so sweet. But you don't need to make that big of a concession. I can certainly relocate to England—after I fulfill my one-year commitment with Cowboy Country USA." She supposed she could talk to her attorney about breaking the contract, although she really didn't want to. "Wait, they still don't try to make the ladies ride sidesaddle in the UK, do they?"

"Of course not, although the English tack is certainly a lot more popular. But don't worry about that. Since I'll be purchasing our own jet soon, I'll be more than happy to cart all your eccentric Western riding equipment back and forth for you."

"Back and forth?"

"Well, I assume that with both of us having commitments in different countries, we'll just make the most of both worlds and spend time in each other's hometowns as needed."

Would she truly be getting the man of her dreams and the travel that she'd always craved? It was more than she could've ever hoped for.

"And don't you worry none about the Broken R," Elmer chimed in before Lady Josephine could rein him back. "Your gram and I will take good care of it while you're sipping tea over yonder with those scone lovers. I've got some big ideas about turning that northern pasture into a drag-racing strip for my hot-rodding club."

"Maybe we should stay in Texas for the time being," Jensen suggested quietly.

"Are you sure?" Amber asked.

"No. But I've discovered that I am quite capable of living with uncertainty—as long as you stay by my side."

"Always."

"I know my mother has ordered champagne to celebrate, but I've taken the liberty to create a private celebration for you later this evening—if you're so inclined."

"I'm definitely up for a private party. What did you have in mind?"

"There's a limousine parked out front, and a hotel suite reserved in Lubbock. I was going to be quite lonely if you would have turned down my proposal."

"I could have never done that, Jensen. You're not just my best friend and lover. You're my soul mate. We were meant to be together."

Then she gave him a kiss that promised him all of her love, for all of her life.

* * * * *

REQUEST YOUR FREE BOOKS!
2 FREE NOVELS PLUS 2 FREE GIFTS!

◈ HARLEQUIN®

SPECIAL EDITION

Life, Love & Family

YES! Please send me 2 FREE Harlequin® Special Edition novels and my 2 FREE gifts (gifts are worth about $10). After receiving them, if I don't wish to receive any more books, I can return the shipping statement marked "cancel." If I don't cancel, I will receive 6 brand-new novels every month and be billed just $4.74 per book in the U.S. or $5.24 per book in Canada. That's a savings of at least 14% off the cover price! It's quite a bargain! Shipping and handling is just 50¢ per book in the U.S. and 75¢ per book in Canada.* I understand that accepting the 2 free books and gifts places me under no obligation to buy anything. I can always return a shipment and cancel at any time. Even if I never buy another book, the two free books and gifts are mine to keep forever.

235/335 HDN F45Y

Name _____
(PLEASE PRINT)

Address _____ Apt. # _____

City _____ State/Prov. _____ Zip/Postal Code _____

Signature (if under 18, a parent or guardian must sign)

Mail to the Harlequin® Reader Service:
IN U.S.A.: P.O. Box 1867, Buffalo, NY 14240-1867
IN CANADA: P.O. Box 609, Fort Erie, Ontario L2A 5X3

Want to try two free books from another line?
Call 1-800-873-8635 or visit www.ReaderService.com.

* Terms and prices subject to change without notice. Prices do not include applicable taxes. Sales tax applicable in N.Y. Canadian residents will be charged applicable taxes. Offer not valid in Quebec. This offer is limited to one order per household. Not valid for current subscribers to Harlequin Special Edition books. All orders subject to credit approval. Credit or debit balances in a customer's account(s) may be offset by any other outstanding balance owed by or to the customer. Please allow 4 to 6 weeks for delivery. Offer available while quantities last.

Your Privacy—The Harlequin® Reader Service is committed to protecting your privacy. Our Privacy Policy is available online at www.ReaderService.com or upon request from the Harlequin Reader Service.

We make a portion of our mailing list available to reputable third parties that offer products we believe may interest you. If you prefer that we not exchange your name with third parties, or if you wish to clarify or modify your communication preferences, please visit us at www.ReaderService.com/consumerschoice or write to us at Harlequin Reader Service Preference Service, P.O. Box 9062, Buffalo, NY 14269. Include your complete name and address.

HSE13R

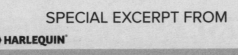
Newly promoted Nathan Garrett is eager to prove he's no longer the company playboy. His assistant, single mom Allison Caldwell, has no interest in helping him with that goal, despite the fiery attraction between them. But as Nate grows closer to Alli's little boy, she wonders whether he might be a family man after all...

Read on for a sneak preview of THE DADDY WISH, by award-winning author Brenda Harlen, the next book in the miniseries THOSE ENGAGING GARRETTS!

***

Allison sipped her wine. Dammit—her pulse was racing and her knees were weak, and there was no way she could sit here beside Nate Garrett, sharing a drink and conversation, and not think about the fact that her tongue had tangled with his.

"I think I'm going to call it a night."

"You haven't finished your wine," he pointed out.

"I'm not much of a drinker."

"Stay," he said.

She lifted her brows. "I don't take orders from you outside the office, Mr. Garrett."

"Sorry—your insistence on calling me 'Mr. Garrett' made me forget that we weren't at the office," he told her. "Please, will you keep me company for a little while?"

"I'm sure there are any number of other women here who will happily keep you company when I'm gone."

"I don't want anyone else's company," he told her.

"Mr. Garrett—"

"Nate."

She sighed. "Why?"

"Because it's my name."

"I meant, why do you want my company?"

"Because I like you," he said simply.

"You don't even know me."

His gaze skimmed down to her mouth, lingered, and she knew he was thinking about the kiss they'd shared. The kiss she hadn't been able to stop thinking about.

"So give me a chance to get to know you," he suggested.

"You'll have that chance when you're in the VP of Finance's office."

She frowned as the bartender, her friend Chelsea, slid a plate of pita bread and spinach dip onto the bar in front of her. "I didn't order this."

"But you want it," Chelsea said, and the wink that followed suggested she was referring to more than the appetizer.

"Actually, I want my bill. It's getting late and…" But her friend had already turned away.

Allison was tempted to walk out and leave Chelsea to pick up the tab, but the small salad she'd made for her own dinner was a distant memory, and she had no willpower when it came to three-cheese spinach dip.

She blew out a breath and picked up a grilled pita triangle. "The service here sucks."

"I've always found that the company of a beautiful woman makes up for many deficiencies."

***

Don't miss THE DADDY WISH by award-winning author Brenda Harlen, the next book in her new miniseries, **THOSE ENGAGING GARRETTS!** *Available February 2015, wherever Harlequin® Special Edition books and ebooks are sold.*
www.Harlequin.com